She could be mistaking sex for love.

That would be female. Foolish. Like her. She had known Simon for less than two weeks. Maybe she was letting loss and loneliness and incredible sex blind her not only to what she had to do but to what she really felt.

But she didn't think so.

She hadn't just fallen for a hunky Mensa millionaire. Okay, the incredible body and amazing mind were a definite plus. But she liked his integrity, his perception, his calm competence and cool humor. She admired the way he took care of others who only wanted to take from him.

No way was she joining their ranks.

She'd come back to the island with Simon tonight because he wasn't safe alone. But her focus had to be on this case. Her self-respect depended on it.

And so could his life.

Dear Reader,

Love is in the air, but the days will certainly be sweeter if you snuggle up with this month's Silhouette Intimate Moments offerings (and a heart-shaped box of decadent chocolates) and let yourself go on the ride of your life! First up, veteran Carla Cassidy dazzles us with *Protecting the Princess*, part of her new miniseries WILD WEST BODYGUARDS. Here, a rugged cowboy rescues a princess and whisks her off to his ranch. What a way to go…!

RITA® Award-winning author Catherine Mann sets our imaginations on fire when she throws together two unlikely lovers in *Explosive Alliance*, the latest book in her popular WINGMEN WARRIORS miniseries. In *Stolen Memory*, the fourth book in her TROUBLE IN EDEN miniseries, stellar storyteller Virginia Kantra tells the tale of a beautiful police officer who sets out to uncover the cause of a powerful man's amnesia. But this supersleuth never expects to fall in love! The second book in her LAST CHANCE HEROES miniseries, *Truly, Madly, Dangerously* by Linda Winstead Jones, plunges us into the lives of a feisty P.I. and protective deputy sheriff who find romance while solving a grisly murder.

Lorna Michaels will touch readers with *Stranger in Her Arms*, in which a caring heroine tends to a rain-battered stranger who shows up on her doorstep. And *Warrior Without a Cause* by Nancy Gideon features a special agent who takes charge when a stalking victim needs his help…and his love.

You won't want to miss this array of roller-coaster reads from Intimate Moments—the line that delivers a charge and a satisfying finish you're sure to savor.

Happy Valentine's Day!

Patience Smith
Associate Senior Editor

Please address questions and book requests to:
Silhouette Reader Service
U.S.: 3010 Walden Ave., P.O. Box 1325, Buffalo, NY 14269
Canadian: P.O. Box 609, Fort Erie, Ont. L2A 5X3

Stolen Memory
VIRGINIA KANTRA

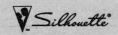

INTIMATE MOMENTS™
Published by Silhouette Books
America's Publisher of Contemporary Romance

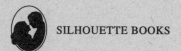 SILHOUETTE BOOKS

ISBN 0-373-27417-3

STOLEN MEMORY

Visit Silhouette Books at www.eHarlequin.com

Printed in U.S.A.

Books by Virginia Kantra

VIRGINIA KANTRA

credits her enthusiasm for strong heroes and courageous heroines to a childhood spent devouring fairy tales. A four-time Romance Writers of America RITA® Award finalist, she has won numerous writing awards, including two National Readers' Choice Awards.

Virginia is married to her college sweetheart, a musician disguised as the owner of a coffeehouse. They make their home in North Carolina with three teenagers, two cats, a dog and various blue-tailed lizards that live under the siding of their house. Her favorite thing to make for dinner? Reservations.

She loves to hear from readers. You can reach her at VirginiaKantra@aol.com or c/o Silhouette Books, 233 Broadway, Suite 1001, New York, NY, 10279.

Special thanks to Lt. A. J. Carter, Criminal Investigation,
Durham Police Department;
to Pam Baustian and Melissa McClone;
and, always, to Michael.

Chapter 1

No man is an island.

But reclusive inventor Simon Ford could afford to buy one. He'd built his modern-day castle on a limestone cliff in the middle of a lake, two miles off-shore from the town of Eden, Illinois.

Detective Laura Baker didn't want to be impressed by Ford's mansion or his money. Which was too bad, because from the inside his multimillion-dollar house was even more imposing than it had looked from the water. She followed Ford's squat, muscled butler—who had a butler anymore? Besides maybe Batman—across the polished stone floor. Soaring wood, jutting stone and wide panes of glass framed the views and let in the light.

Jeez. Her entire apartment would fit inside Ford's foyer.

Laura resisted the urge to wipe her hands on her uniform pants and stuffed them in her pockets instead. This could be considered a crime scene. She wasn't about to contaminate it by touching anything. Besides, the butler guy was watching her like he expected her to make a grab for the family silver or something.

He lumbered in front of her to a broad, shallow staircase that spilled down to a room lined with windows and furnished in natural woods and neutrals. A massive fireplace split the view. The only spot of color in the room, a violent collision of oranges, purples and reds over the mantel, seemed jarringly out of place.

Silhouetted against the sparkling lake was a big, dark, solitary figure. Ford?

Something about him—the powerful line of his back, maybe, or the rigid set of his shoulders—brought Laura to attention. Beneath her heavy Kevlar vest, her heart beat faster.

Stupid. She was not impressed, she reminded herself. She would not be intimidated. She touched her elbow to the gun at her waist for reassurance.

Her guide stopped at the top of the stairs and scowled. "The police are here."

"Thank you, Quinn." The tall figure didn't turn around. "I'll call you when we're done."

Quinn shot Laura a resentful look. She returned it blandly. As the only female on Eden's small police force, she was used to men who considered her presence an invasion of their turf.

"Right," Quinn said, and stomped away.

Ford pivoted from the glass. His head lifted sharply. "You're not Chief Denko."

Good deduction. The man should have been a detective.

"Detective Baker," Laura said.

"Simon Ford." He surveyed her a moment, silently. With the light behind him, she couldn't see his face.

A disadvantage, she thought, and wondered if he'd positioned himself deliberately.

"I asked for Chief Denko," he said.

And whatever the almighty Simon Ford asked for, Laura gathered from that deep, abrupt voice, the almighty Simon Ford got.

Except this time.

She kept her cop mask firmly in place. "It's Memorial Day weekend, Mr. Ford. We see a lot of traffic and handle a lot of calls over the holidays." *Which you would know if you ever bothered to get involved in the community.* "Chief Denko was called to an accident scene."

A pileup on Highway 12 that had pulled patrol cars and snarled traffic for miles. She was missing all the excitement.

"But you are a detective?"

"That's right," she said, doing her best not to sound defensive. Her rank was very new. She'd completed her training with the district attorney's office in Fox Hole less than six months ago.

"Then why are you in uniform?"

Laura frowned. Somehow this interview had gotten turned around. He shouldn't be the one asking questions.

"In a small department like ours, detectives have to be prepared to do double duty. And most tourists respond better to an officer in uniform." Not that her uniform seemed to be having a similar effect on Ford. She cleared her throat. "The dispatcher said you had a situation out here?"

"Yes." He didn't elaborate.

She waited. Maybe now that Ford had a detective on site, he regretted calling. It happened. Somebody claimed an item was stolen and then discovered they'd misplaced it. Or got pissed off at a neighbor's kids and then relented. A lot of police work wasn't solving crimes but soothing tempers. Civil assists, the chief called them, but he was adamant his officers respond to every call with professional attention.

"You want to tell me about it?" Laura invited.

Ford studied her, still with his back to the light. And then he said, abruptly, "My lab was broken into."

All righty. Now they were getting somewhere. Break-ins were unfortunately common at the luxury homes around the lake. Laura could deal with a break-in. Although any local punk who breached Ford's island fortress had to be crazy or lucky or both.

She took out her notebook, grateful to have something to do with her hands. "Here?"

Ford inclined his head. "Downstairs."

"When?"

"Two days ago."

She lifted her pen. "And you've just now discovered it?"

"No. I was here when it occurred."

She felt her brows pull together and consciously smoothed her expression. "Why don't you explain to me what happened," she said.

"Why don't we sit down first," Ford countered. He took a step forward, into the light from a side window, so that she got her first good look at his face.

Oh, boy. Oh, man. She felt the punch of sexual attraction like a blow to her midsection. *This* was Simon Ford? The geeky inventor? The soft-living millionaire?

It just went to show her the chief was right. A good detective should never theorize ahead of her facts.

He looked like something out of her adolescent fantasies, a warrior poet or a priest king. Not that Laura believed in fairy tales anymore. His face was cold, strong and striking. Guarded, she thought. His dark hair—longer than she usually liked—fell over his forehead. His eyes were cool as rain.

They narrowed on her, and she felt again that odd prickle like a warning on the back of her neck. "Have we met?" he asked.

"I don't think so."

"Are you sure? You look…"

She didn't want to think about how she looked with her ball cap jammed over her untidy braid and sweat stains under her arms. The boat ride over had been windy and rough.

"Familiar?" she provided.

"No. As if you recognized me."

"Nope." She shook her head. From another man she might have suspected a pickup line. But Ford's voice was perfectly dispassionate. His face gave nothing away. "Sorry."

He continued to study her with those disconcertingly light gray eyes, plainly unconvinced.

Annoyance sharpened her voice. "Look, if we'd met, you'd remember."

"Not necessarily."

They hardly ran in the same circles. Hell, they barely inhabited the same town. Ford kept himself to himself. He even did his grocery shopping in Chicago, well over an hour away. It hadn't endeared him any to the local merchants.

"You have a problem with your memory?" Laura asked dryly.

Ford smiled a small, wintry smile. "Actually, yes. I do."

Her eyes widened. She had to watch her mouth. She was off balance, reacting emotionally, like some stupid traffic officer letting a pretty woman flirt her way out of a ticket.

There was no quicker way for a cop to get into trouble.

"Maybe we better sit down after all," she said, making a grab for the situation. "And you can tell me why you called."

Could he? Simon wondered.

Doubt hammered inside his chest and seized his head in a vise. He'd expected a seasoned police chief to respond to his call, not this young, wary female. He didn't want her. But he was attracted to her.

Was she his type? He didn't even know. She was as lean and graceful as a greyhound, with a narrow, intense face and a wide, mobile mouth. Her light brown gaze was clear and direct.

She looked honest. She might even be competent. But he couldn't rely on his own judgment. For all he knew, he was a lousy judge of character.

He hesitated, his head pounding.

Her mouth quirked. "Or we can stand."

Her humor tipped the scales in her favor. He couldn't trust anyone who worked for him. Why not a total stranger?

"We'll sit," he said.

He lowered himself cautiously onto one of the cordovan leather couches flanking the fireplace. Sudden movement, he'd discovered, hurt his head.

Detective Baker sat, too, her back straight beneath her bulky vest and ugly uniform.

Simon opened his mouth. But he still didn't know how to begin.

His vacillation, his helplessness, infuriated him. Was he always like this? God, he hoped not.

"So." Detective Baker regarded him expectantly, her notebook open on her knee. "You called the station."

And now he was questioning even the wisdom of that idea.

But after more than twenty-four hours of groping and bumbling in a fog, Simon had reluctantly acknowledged he couldn't cope on his own. He needed professional help.

Fear clawed him. *Yeah, like a psychiatrist.*

He took a deep breath for calm. "On Wednesday night, I left the corporate headquarters in Chicago and came here."

Detective Baker nodded. "Alone?"

"No, I was accompanied by one of my security staff." Or

so he'd been told. "We left the office at seven, which means we would have arrived on the island no later than seven-thirty."

Her brows arched. "You must have broken some speed limits."

He didn't smile. "We took the company helicopter." He'd been told that, too.

"I've seen it." She scribbled something. "Who was your pilot?"

"I flew myself." He told himself he wasn't trying to impress her. Just as well, because her expression never flickered.

"Okay, so you got here at seven-thirty and found...what?"

Simon teetered on the edge of self-revelation, an enormous chasm that yawned at his feet and threatened to swallow him.

He took a step back. "Everything must have been in order then. I know I made dinner." There had been dishes in the dishwasher the next morning and fresh vegetables in the stainless-steel refrigerator.

"And then?"

"I went down to the lab."

"Did you have a reason?"

"What do you mean?"

"Did something attract your attention?"

"I don't know." He closed his teeth on the thin edge of desperation he heard fracturing his voice. "I don't think so. I may simply have intended to get some work done after dinner."

"'May have.'"

"My company—Lumen Corp—has several new projects in development. Laser research." He could say that with some certainty now. He'd spent hours yesterday fighting off pain and despair, searching for clues on the Internet and in the house, struggling to make sense of the equipment and files downstairs. The scope of his loss still stunned him. He needed to trust her, to tell her exactly how serious his situation was. But pride and panic constricted his chest and tightened his throat. "I must have been working on one of them when I was interrupted."

"'Interrupted,'" she repeated without inflection.

It wasn't quite a question. It stopped short of actual challenge. But he was insecure enough to bristle. "I presume so."

He was relieved when she appeared to let it go. "Okay. So, you were downstairs working in your lab and…what happened?"

His brief relief evaporated. "That's the problem. I don't know. I must have lost consciousness when I was attacked. When I came to, I was staring up at the ceiling with a bump on my head and a whopping big headache."

"Mr. Ford." Her voice was soothing. Her eyes were sharp. "Is it possible you fell? It was late. You mentioned you'd had a meal, maybe some wine…"

Simon's hands curled into fists. If he shouted at her, she'd really think he was a nut job. "The bump is on the side of my skull, Detective." He slid his fingers into the hair above his ear to show her. "I was lying on my back."

"But you don't remember how you got there."

"No." He couldn't delay confession any longer. He drew another deep breath. "I don't remember anything around the time of the attack."

He didn't remember anything, period.

Oh, he had some basic stuff down. He could dress and feed himself, turn on the lights and dishwasher. If he didn't stop to analyze how he did it, he could even operate the TV and computer.

But he had no knowledge of who he was or what he did or how the hell he was supposed to continue doing it.

The detective blinked, once. "You mean you have amnesia?"

She didn't believe him. "Amnesia can be a product of head trauma," Simon said stiffly.

"Is that what your doctor told you?"

"No. I looked it up on the Internet."

His computer, thank God, had been up and running when he'd searched his office. He hadn't dared to turn it off, since he had no idea if his files were password protected.

She laid her pen flat on her notebook. "Mr. Ford, I'll be happy to take your statement. I can take a look around, talk to your security people, check for signs of forced entry. You have surveillance cameras, right? But I really think you need to see a doctor."

She didn't understand.

He hadn't explained himself clearly.

Frustration made him abrupt. "That's the last thing I need."

"Excuse me?"

"I told you, my company is in the process of launching new laser technology. I can't have my competitors—I can't have people in my own company—thinking I've lost it."

"But doctor/patient privilege—"

"It would still get out I'd seen a doctor. Someone is bound to ask why. I can't afford any weakness."

"Why not?"

She probably thought the bump on the head had made him paranoid. But he wasn't. He knew he wasn't. He felt the sharp certainty of threat, the only tangible guidepost in the fog that was his brain.

And he couldn't explain that to her without sounding even more crazy.

"Look," he said, using really basic concepts and small words she could understand, "Wednesday night somebody got into my lab and hit me over the head and robbed me."

"You were robbed."

She was doing that echo thing again.

Simon set his jaw. "Yes."

"Are you sure? I mean, if you can't remember…"

"The safe was open," he snapped.

Now—finally!—she picked up her pen. "And do you have a record of the safe's contents?" she asked, still plainly humoring him.

"There's got to be a list somewhere." His notes were precise and methodical. His desk was ruthlessly systematized, his bedroom uncluttered. Everything he'd seen pointed to his being an orderly, organized, painstaking individual. He must have kept an inventory of something as important as the contents of his safe. He just hadn't found it yet.

"It would help if you could locate it," said the detective practically. "Where was your security guard during this attack and robbery?"

He stared at her.

"You said he came up with you from Chicago," she reminded him gently. "He showed me in. Mr. Quinn?"

Simon shook his head, forgetting his resolution to avoid sudden movements. Pain momentarily grayed his vision and robbed him of breath.

When he could speak again, he said, "Not Quinn. Quinn Brown is my household manager. Apparently he was visiting his daughter for a few days. He arrived yesterday."

Simon calculated he'd been alone at that point for almost twenty-four hours and conscious for five or six. He hadn't recognized his employee's face. He hadn't recognized his own name, either, when Quinn had called him, except that it had appeared on the various notes and papers he'd found.

It had been a relief, he remembered, to realize that it was his name, that this must be his house.

Some sense of self-preservation, a horror of weakness or

perception of danger, had kept him from confessing his confusion and utter helplessness to his household manager.

The same instinct made him cautious now.

"The guard was supposed to stay at the house until Quinn returned. But when Quinn came to work, no one was here."

Detective Baker frowned. "Except you."

Simon inclined his head in careful acknowledgment. "Except me."

She tapped her pen on her notebook. "Doors and windows?"

At least she appeared to be taking him seriously. "Locked. And the security system in the house was on."

"The safe?"

"Open. Either someone else knew the combination—which seems unlikely—or I opened it myself. I could have been putting away my notes for the day when I was interrupted."

"I'll take a look at it," she said. "This other guard—have you tried to reach him? Who's in charge of your company security?"

He didn't know. "I thought it best to contact the police."

She caught his implication immediately. "You think it was an inside job."

Simon was grateful for her quick understanding. But he didn't answer her directly. "I don't know."

"Isn't there anyone you can trust?"

He didn't know that either. He'd searched the office and the master bedroom for clues. Nothing. On his dresser sat a framed photo of a teenage girl with a row of silver earrings whose eyes were the same shape as the ones he saw in his mirror. His daughter? But then why didn't she live with him? There were several bedrooms upstairs, but no magazines, no makeup, no feminine clutter. Only a bikini, forgotten in the back of a drawer, and some half-empty bottles of shampoo and conditioner stashed under a sink suggested he sometimes had visitors.

His apparent isolation was frightening. He must have friends and family. Perhaps a woman? But they had left no trace in his life.

What kind of a man was he?

The detective was still waiting for his answer, watching him with what was certainly only professional concern in her eyes. Or impatience.

Isn't there anyone you can trust?

He wanted to trust her. But was that because she was trustworthy or because he was desperate for connection, eager to imprint on the first person he saw like a baby duck? The idea revolted him.

"That's what we need to find out," he said.

She tilted her head. "That's going to be tough if you can't remember who attacked you."

Even tougher if he didn't tell her the whole truth. But how could he?

"Amnesia is usually a temporary condition," he offered instead.

"How temporary?"

She was persistent. He admired that, even if it was inconvenient. He shrugged. "A few seconds to a few weeks. I have been able to recall everything since I regained consciousness. My short-term memory is unaffected."

"Great. So if I come back tomorrow you'll recognize me."

Startled, he met her gaze. Her mouth indented at the corners. She was joking, he realized in relief. He smiled back cautiously.

"So, this guard, the one who came with you from Chicago…" Detective Baker flipped a page in her notebook, all business again. "What was his name?"

"Swirsky." It had meant nothing to him when Quinn had told him. "Pete Swirsky."

Her notebook slid from her knee and hit the floor with a crack. She leaned forward to pick it up. When she straightened at last, her face was a deep, unbecoming red.

"Is anything the matter?" Simon asked.

"I… No, I…" She fussed with the crumpled pages on her lap. "Sorry."

He sat back, fascinated by the sudden change in her demeanor. "Take your time."

"I'm fine," she said, a little too sharply. "He's missing, you said?"

"He wasn't here when Quinn returned. I don't know when—or how—he left."

"Have to be by boat. Someone may have seen him. Anyway, since he works for you it shouldn't be much trouble to track him down." Her voice was brisk and practical. But her fingers, as she smoothed the pages of her notebook, trembled slightly. "In the meantime, I'll need a statement from Mr. Brown and a look at your lab. Has anyone been in there since your…accident?"

Accident? How about "attack"? Or "assault"? Some other a-word that indicated she'd accepted his story.

But maybe he was hoping for too much. At least she was going to investigate.

Which raised another problem.

"As far as I know, I'm the only one with any reason to go in there."

Her brows flicked up. "Really? Who mops your floors?"

He didn't know. "A cleaning service?"

"Right." She made another note. "I'll talk to Mr. Brown."

Despite her lack of inflection, Simon felt dismissed. Disparaged. Why? Because his memory loss made him useless to her? Or because he hadn't considered something so basic as the people who must work for him?

"What will you tell him?" he asked.

"I'll want to know who cleans for you. What their schedule is, if they have keys to the house and the lab. Stuff like that."

"I meant, what are you going to tell him about me?"

"About your memory loss."

He liked that she met his gaze directly. "Yes."

"Well… It's not a crime to forget things. Otherwise, I'd have to arrest half the population of the Sunset Pines Retirement Community." He was pretty sure this time she was kidding. "You really think it would hurt your business if it got out you had this temporary amnesia thing?"

"Yes," he said baldly. "The value of this company depends on my research ability. Mental aberration is not reassuring to stockholders."

"You have bigger worries right now than your investors. Once it gets out that you're walking around, whoever attacked you is going to worry you'll identify him."

If was the first sign she'd given that she believed he'd been attacked. Something inside Simon relaxed.

"I was struck on the side of the head, probably as I was turning around," he offered. "It's likely I never saw him."

"He may not care. He hit you once. Do you really want to risk him coming back to finish the job?"

"I'll take my chances."

She scowled. "Don't take too many. You sure you won't see a doctor?"

"Sure."

"Well, it's your—"

He was almost certain she was going to say "funeral."

"—skull," she said. "Concussions can tire you out, though. You should try to get plenty of rest."

Her concern, however professional, made Simon feel

slightly less isolated. He had been up most of last night trying to find an answer to the puzzles that plagued him. The
night before he'd spent lying on the cold floor of the lab. He
was strained, exhausted and aching in every muscle.

But of course he couldn't tell her that.

"Thank you," he said gravely. "I will."

She hesitated as if she wanted to say something more and
then shrugged. "I left my field kit on the boat. I'll go get it,
and then I'll talk to your guy, Brown, and poke around."

He watched her slim, straight figure climb the stairs and
cross the echoing hall. She was leaving. He was alone.

Simon had the uncomfortable sense he was often alone.

But this time, this once, he didn't like it at all.

Chapter 2

"I don't know what to think," Laura said honestly to her boss when he called her into his office late the following day. It was a Saturday, but they both were working. Chief Denko, because his personal life was admirably organized, and Laura, because it was her shift and she had no personal life.

"Ford definitely has a bump on the head," she continued. "But I didn't find any tool marks or fingerprints to support his claim of a break-in. We don't even know for sure that a crime took place. He could have emptied the safe himself as part of an insurance scam."

She didn't mention Ford's claim, that the bump on his head had affected his brain.

And as for Ford's suspicion that it was an inside job, that the guard that night had attacked and robbed him before disappearing… Her stomach tied itself in knots. Nope, she definitely didn't want to go there.

Not that she had a choice. She had a duty. And Police Chief Jarek Denko would demand a complete and impartial investigation in any case.

"Has Ford filed an insurance claim?" he asked.

"No," Laura admitted.

Chief Denko regarded her levelly from the other side of his utilitarian gray metal desk, his hands folded on the stained blotter. The Eden town council didn't believe in spending money on fancy furniture for its public servants. But somehow they'd scraped together enough sense and an appropriate salary to hire Denko, a former homicide detective from Chicago's notorious Area 3, as their chief of police.

After the last two Bozos who'd held that the position, Laura respected the lean, harsh-featured police chief enormously. She dreaded letting him down.

Denko steepled his fingers. "No signs of forced entry, you said?"

"No, sir."

"Who has keys to the house?"

"No keys. Entry is controlled by magnetic passcards and internal bolts operating on a tiered code system. Only the highest access codes get you into the house itself."

"And who has those codes?"

"I've requested a complete list from the security company. But the guy on the phone said the master passcards were reserved for security personnel and Ford himself."

Denko tapped the pages on the blotter in front of him. "Your report says the tapes are missing from the security cameras. They weren't simply disabled?"

Laura shook her head. "Vandalizing the cameras would have set off the alarm automatically. So either the intruder knew where the cameras were and how they operated, or there was no intruder and someone on the inside swiped the tapes to avoid being identified."

"Ford?" Denko suggested. "That would fit your insurance fraud theory."

But once her chief put it into words, Laura found she didn't like her theory anymore.

Isn't there anyone you can trust?

That's what we need to find out.

Simon Ford had trusted her. Or he was playing her for a fool. Neither possibility sat comfortably with her right now.

"Maybe the tapes aren't missing. Maybe his security people forgot to load the cameras," she offered without conviction.

Denko raised his eyebrows. "The same day Ford calls to report a break-in? But you can ask, by all means. Who installed his security system?"

"A private contractor—Executive Corporate Industrial Protection."

"E.C.I.P.?"

"You've heard of them?" She shouldn't be surprised. In Illinois law enforcement, Jarek Denko was like God, all-knowing and damn near all-powerful.

"They hire a lot of ex-cops," he explained with a slight smile. "Military, too. Do they provide the personnel or just the system?"

"According to Quinn Brown, they provide complete security for Lumen Corp. That includes the house and the Chicago headquarters."

"So the bodyguard, Brown, is one of theirs?"

"Household manager, sir. And no. He reports directly to Ford. He's been with him for the past nine years. Took a couple of days off to visit his daughter. The timing is suspicious, but we can confirm his alibi easily enough."

"What about the other man? Swirsky? Do you have a lead on him yet?"

Her stomach twisted again like wet rope. Her palms were damp. "He is an E.C.I.P. employee. He was scheduled to go on vacation next week. The company is cooperating, but I haven't been able to reach him by phone yet. I thought I'd try him at his apartment in Chicago."

"Family?" Denko asked.

She hesitated, her heart thumping. "Swirsky has a son living in Chicago. I left a message, but he hasn't returned my call yet."

"All right. Let me know when you hear something. And get that list of the safe's contents from Ford." Denko gave her a brief nod and pulled another file toward him.

She was dismissed.

Laura cleared her throat. "There's, uh, one other thing you should probably know that's not in my report."

The chief looked up from his file.

"Peter Swirsky…the missing guard?" She braced her shoulders. "He's my father."

Denko froze. "The hell he is."

She rushed to explain. "It's not a conflict of interest. We haven't spoken in years. I wouldn't even have brought it up, except—"

"Except if you hadn't and I found out about it, I'd have your ass," Denko said.

She winced. "I can promise you, it won't affect my ability to do my job at all."

"You're right. It won't. I'm reassigning this case to Palmer."

Dan Palmer was the detective on the swing shift, 2:00 p.m. to midnight. Laura liked him—respected him, even—but for reasons she wasn't prepared to examine, she didn't want this case snatched away.

"I conducted the investigation of the scene," she argued. "I interviewed Ford. I can remain impartial. I can…"

Get her father to talk to her? Hardly. She hadn't been able to accomplish that in ten years.

She switched tactics. "Let Dan take Swirsky's statement. One interview. I don't have a problem with that."

"If it stops at one interview," Denko said. "What if we establish that a crime was committed? What if Swirsky becomes a suspect?"

"It'll never happen," she said with conviction.

"Why not?"

"Because he'd never commit a crime. Pete Swirsky doesn't break the rules. He doesn't even bend them."

He never deviated, never doubted, never forgave. His inflexibility made him a lousy father. But it didn't make him a suspect.

"People change," Denko observed.

She certainly had. But the old man never would.

"Then I'll live with that," she said. "Let me do my job, sir."

The chief rubbed his jaw with his thumb. "'Swirsky,' huh?"

"Maiden name. I was married. Briefly."

Nine weeks. That's how long it had taken her to figure out she'd made the second biggest mistake of her life. But by the time her marriage to Tommy Baker ended, her estrangement from her father was complete.

"Good Polish name," the chief said.

Laura relaxed a fraction. She was forgiven, then. "Yes, sir."

"All right, thank you," Denko said. "You did a good job processing the scene. But you're off the case. Turn your notes over to Palmer."

She owed him.

Laura gripped the wheel of the battered police boat as it chugged across the lake. She didn't owe him her loyalty. Or even an explanation. But the memory of Simon Ford's clear, light eyes lingered at the back of her mind like a question. She couldn't shake the feeling that she owed him…something.

A warning, maybe. Or a goodbye.

Around her, the water teemed with inner tubes and motor boats, wind surfers and sails, as tourists and townspeople took advantage of the three-day weekend. She was working harbor patrol, answering radio calls for service, checking permits and boating licenses, keeping an eye out for inebriated fishermen and inexperienced sailors.

When she was a rookie, Laura used to bust her hump on patrol. As if the number of citations she wrote for open alcohol containers or out-of-date landing permits somehow proved she was the baddest, best cop on the force.

She knew better now. Good cops didn't get hung up on busy work when a fellow officer requested backup on the other side of the lake. But a discretionary detour to Angel Island wouldn't interfere with her doing her job.

She hoped.

The wind tugged at the curled brim of her EPD ball cap. She set her feet against the swell of a passing speedboat. Behind her, the marina faded to a smudge of red brick and gray shingles. The town slid away to her left, the spire of St. Raphael's Catholic Church like a mast against the horizon.

Her heartbeat quickened as she headed out to open water. Nerves, she told herself firmly. It had to be nerves. It certainly wasn't anticipation at seeing Ford again.

His private pier jutted into the water, aggressively new, the treated wood standing out like dental work against the tumbled shore. Laura looped a line around a post and hopped onto the dock, ignoring the posted warning: No Trespassing. Shrugging, she started up the service road that wound through the trees to the house.

A surly Quinn answered the door and stomped ahead of

her up the steps to Ford's office. Climbing the long, curving staircase made Laura feel like she was in some fairy tale, braving the tower to rescue the princess. Except she made a lousy Prince Charming.

And the man at the top of the stairs was definitely no Sleeping Beauty.

He hunched over his desk, a wide slab of pale, polished wood. The light from the surrounding windows cast his face in light and shadow: his deep, focused eyes, his cheeks carved with concentration, his mouth fixed in a determined line. He looked like a wizard king brooding over the fate of his kingdom.

Laura gave herself a mental shake. This was no time for her to develop a fantasy life. She'd spent too many years fighting the prejudices of her male colleagues and her own feelings to get all moony-eyed and stupid now.

Stuffing her hands in her pockets, she glanced around the room. She'd climbed up here the day before, testing locks, checking for broken windows. It was all spare lines and blank surfaces. Outside, the lake sparkled with light and life. But inside, the walls sealed out all sound. Despite the sun that poured through the glass, the air was cold.

Quinn's voice dropped into the silence like a rock on an ice-filmed puddle. "It's Baker. She's back."

Ford's concentration broke. He blinked at her, recalled from his spell.

"I, uh… Sorry," Laura said. "I didn't mean to interrupt your—" What did he do? Laser research. Good God. "—your work."

He raised his hand, palm out. Cutting off her apologies? Or dismissing Quinn? The butler tromped back downstairs.

"You're not interrupting," Ford said. He rubbed the bridge of his nose, as if he was tired. She squelched her instinctive sympathy. "And I'm not working. Any news?"

I'm off the case.

That's what she'd come to tell him. But when she opened her mouth, what actually came out was, "So, what are you doing?"

"I'm writing a computer program that will let me hack into my own system and create a new password."

"Oh." Right. She'd forgotten he was a freaking genius. He definitely didn't need her pity. "Sounds complicated."

He smiled faintly. "Not particularly. Most hacking is a simple matter of repeating steps that exploit common system weaknesses."

"Simple, huh? How long have you been at it?"

"A few hours," he admitted.

Reluctant admiration stirred. "You don't give up easily, do you?"

"No." His remote, light eyes studied her a moment. "Not when there's something I want."

Her heart went *ka-thump.* Stupid, she scolded herself. He didn't mean her. And she didn't want him.

She frowned, struck by something he'd said. "Why do you need a new password?"

"I'm updating my computer's security."

"Okay, fine, but…why would you need to hack into your system to do that?"

He didn't answer.

"You didn't—" Laura pressed her lips together. Okay, now she really was being stupid. But she had to ask. "You didn't forget your password, did you? When you got hit on the head?"

His expression never flickered. Maybe he hadn't lost his memory. Maybe she was losing her mind.

But Simon Ford wasn't the only one who didn't give up easily. She wasn't going to let embarrassment or attraction put her off doing her job.

"You said you couldn't remember the attack."

He inclined his head. "That's correct."

"What else?"

"Excuse me?"

He was stalling. She was sure of it. Nobody talked in that ultra-formal way unless he was either a snob and a smart-ass or stalling. Simon Ford might live in a castle and have a genius IQ, but he hadn't done anything yet to make her think he was a snob. Or a smart-ass.

She ran through their interview in her head, trying to fit her new theory to snatches of their conversation.

"What else don't you remember?" she asked.

He looked at her quizzically. "If I knew that, then I wouldn't have forgotten it, would I?"

She scowled, rethinking the smart-ass bit.

"Never mind." Not her problem, she told herself. Not even her case. She needed to depersonalize. "I came to tell you I'm off the case."

Simon's dark brows drew together over his perfect nose. "What?"

"Chief Denko reassigned your case to Detective Palmer. He'll be out to talk with you tomorrow. Tell him whatever you want."

"Why are you off the case?"

He sounded annoyed, which for some perverse reason made her feel better. Not enough to confide in him, but enough to be reassuring.

"You'll like Palmer," she said. "He has experience."

"I want you," Ford said.

She ignored the little thrill his words gave her. He didn't mean it like that. "Well, you can't have me. I told you. The chief gave your case to Palmer."

"I want you," Ford repeated, unsmiling and intent, and her pulse kicked up a notch.

"Very nice," approved an amused male voice from behind her. "Does she come with the handcuffs?"

Laura jerked around.

A preppie god in a white silk shirt with the sleeves rolled back lounged in the doorway, smiling at her with lazy charm. Tall, blond and very handsome. If Simon Ford was the Wizard King, then this dude was Prince Charming. No wonder she'd felt miscast on her way up the stairs.

Quinn Brown spoke up from behind him. "Your brother's here, Mr. Ford."

Laura turned back to the desk and pinned Ford with an accusing look. "You have a brother?"

He had a brother.

Simon sat and absorbed the shock, trying to keep it from his face. After three days of being alone except for his household manager, it should have been reassuring to discover he had some family. But he felt no instant connection. No recognition. Nothing at all.

The younger man stepped forward, extending his hand. "Dylan Ford."

"Laura Baker."

Not "Detective," Simon noted. Her name was Laura.

"Nice to meet you." Dylan smiled, revealing perfect teeth against his perfect tan. "I didn't know Simon had a thing for women in uniform."

Perfect jackass, Simon thought.

"Detective Baker is here to investigate the break-in," he said coolly.

The smile faded. "'Break-in'? Here? When?"

He sounded more startled than concerned.

"Wednesday night, we believe," Simon said.

"Before you got in?"

So his brother kept some track of his whereabouts.

"No," said Simon, watching him closely. "After."

"Wow." Dylan ran a hand through his perfectly styled hair. "Did you see anything?"

He didn't ask if Simon had been hurt. Maybe it was a natural omission. The bump on his head wasn't obvious. Presumably the only person who even knew he'd been attacked was the one who'd struck him.

"Not really," he said.

"What did they take? TV? Stereo?"

"Nothing like that." He glanced at Laura Baker, wondering how much he should say, but she was still staring at his tall, blond, handsome brother. "The safe was open."

Dylan swore. "They didn't get the rubies, did they?"

Laura Baker's attention snapped back like a rubber band. Simon could practically feel her vibrating.

"I believe they did," he said slowly. "The safe was empty."

"Damn it, Simon, I told you I had the people from Vulcan Gemstones lined up to look at them this week."

He had no idea what the younger man was talking about. "Sorry. I forgot."

"Of course you did," Dylan said bitterly. "You didn't care about my plans anyway. All you care about is the damn technological applications."

"If you mean my laser research…" Simon said cautiously.

"Of course I mean your laser research. Those rubies could be so much more than a byproduct. But you never understood their significance outside of the lab."

"Probably not," Simon agreed.

"I certainly don't," Laura said. "Are you saying you kept rubies in your lab?"

"Solid-state lasers use synthetic ruby rods to emit energy in a specific wavelength," explained Simon. It felt good to know something. "Basically chromium doped aluminum oxide of a higher purity and quality than natural gemstones. Some of my research has focused on new methods for creating those rods."

She blinked. "You mean, you make fakes?"

"Cultured gemstones," Dylan corrected. "Simon developed a flux growth process that creates crystals without bubbles or thermal strain lines. And the depth of color is amazing. With the proper cutting and machining, his rubies are virtually undetectable from natural stones."

"And they're missing," Laura said.

"Apparently," Simon said.

All that research, lost. With his memory gone, how long would it take him to retrace his steps, to duplicate his work?

"How much?" she asked Simon.

"Excuse me?"

"How much were they worth?"

"The investment in time alone—"

Dylan laughed shortly. "You're asking the wrong man, sweetheart. He had over a hundred stones stashed in that safe at slightly over a carat each. Vivid saturation. Almost no inclusions. I'd say we're looking at a market value of almost half a million dollars."

"But they're paste, right?" Laura asked. "I mean, they're good quality, but they're still fakes."

Dylan shook his head. "Chemically, those rubies are identical to the real deal. There's not one jeweler in ten who could tell them apart. Which is why getting the patents and developing a marketing strategy is so important."

"It's irrelevant," Simon said. "We're not in the business of selling jewelry."

"You're not in the business of selling jewelry," his brother shot back.

"And it's my business."

A nasty little silence fell.

Simon wondered if most of his conversations with his brother ended this way. If so, it would certainly explain why Dylan hadn't called.

His pleasant face set. "You did agree to let Vulcan at least examine the stones," he said tightly.

Did he? He could have. He didn't remember.

"So, what's the problem?" Simon asked.

"The *problem* is they're missing," Dylan said, his voice rising. "And I've got to wonder— Ah, hell." He broke off, again thrusting his hand through his hair.

"Do you think your brother is complicit in the stones' disappearance?" Laura asked.

She was supposed to be on his side, damn it. He wanted her on his side. Her question caught him like a whack across the shins.

But it didn't trip his brother at all.

"No, I don't. Of course I don't," Dylan said. "But it's hard to see how else this could have happened. This place has better security than the airport." He wheeled to face Simon. "What about Quinn? Did he see anything?"

He sounded interested. Eager. Innocent?

Or anxious to divert the blame to someone else?

Cold settled in the pit of Simon's stomach. He didn't know enough about his brother or their relationship to even guess.

"He wasn't with me that night," Simon said.

"You mean they let you out without a keeper?"

"One of the guards came with me from Chicago."

"So where was he?"

Simon breathed in deeply. He had to say something. Something intelligent, something that wouldn't betray his loss of memory.

"Pete Swirsky is being sought for questioning at this time," Laura said, unexpectedly coming to his rescue.

"Does that mean you think he did it?" Dylan asked.

The detective's slim body stiffened. "It means he's being sought for questioning."

"What do you mean, sought?"

"According to E.C.I.P., he was scheduled to go on vacation this week," Laura said. "He hasn't reported for work since Wednesday."

"So, he just happens to go missing at the same time as the rubies?" Dylan shook his head. "I don't think so. It's been four days. Why haven't the police picked him up yet?"

Because they hadn't known about the rubies until now.

They hadn't known because Simon didn't remember.

And Simon didn't trust his own brother enough to tell him so.

He searched Dylan's fair, handsome face as if it held the clue to their estrangement. Why didn't he trust him? What else didn't he remember? Was the fault in Dylan or in Simon himself?

He waited for Laura to say something, to defend herself and her department against his brother's criticism.

But all she said was, "The police are pursuing every available lead at this time."

"So how come you haven't found him yet? It's not like there are a lot of places to hide in a town this size."

Her eyes narrowed. "Swirsky lives in Chicago."

"So put the Chicago police on it."

"It's not their jurisdiction."

"Yeah, but at least they'd get the job done."

Anger whipped through Simon.

"Back off. I made the call. It was my call to make."

The certainty in his own voice surprised him.

But his brother appeared to take it in stride. "Yeah, that's what you always say." He gave Laura a long look up and down. "I guess I can't blame you for wanting to keep her around. Let me know if you find anything."

He strolled out.

Laura watched him go, her chin up and her hands in her pockets. Simon could see the outline of her knuckles through the shiny blue fabric.

"Son of a bitch," Simon said.

She jerked one shoulder in a shrug. "Don't worry about it. I'm the only female officer on a small-town police force. I've pretty much heard it all before."

He admired her self-possession. But Dylan's chauvinistic attitude irked him. "Not from my brother."

"You're not responsible for what he says."

"Aren't I?"

He didn't know. He felt he should be.

She faced him squarely. "Listen, I've got a kid brother, too. And God help us both if I tried to take responsibility for him."

Her gaze was clear and direct as a punch. He felt its impact in his gut, harder than recognition, deeper than desire. His breath went.

How long they stood there, staring at each other, he didn't know.

But then her thin face colored. She looked away, breaking their connection. "I've got to go."

His heart was pounding, his chest felt tight, and he hadn't touched her, hadn't kissed her, hadn't… What the hell had just happened here? He didn't need his memory back to recognize lust. But this understanding was both more foreign and more seductive.

"Go where?" he asked. "What are you planning to do?"

"I'm on harbor patrol today."

"I meant about Swirsky."

"Nothing. I'm off the case."

"No." His protest was automatic. Instinctive. "I want you to handle the investigation."

"It's not up to you." Her mouth quirked ruefully. "Or me, either. Chief Denko has assigned the case to Detective Palmer."

That long look had diverted the blood from his brain to below his belt. He couldn't think worth a damn. Which explained what he said next.

"I'll pay you."

She stiffened. "For what?"

All right, he'd said it badly. But it wasn't such a bad idea. Laura Baker was intelligent. Stubborn. Discreet. She hadn't blurted out his loss of memory to his brother. She'd come to him directly to tell him about the new detective assigned to the case. And she had nothing personal at stake in the outcome of this investigation.

"I want someone close to me I can trust." Pushing back from his computer, he stood. "I want to hire you."

She shook her head. "I can't work for you."

He came around his desk. "Why not?"

Her soft lips set. "Well, for one thing, I already have a job."

Her resistance made him want her more. He didn't take time to reflect on what that revealed about his character.

"You can do it in your off hours," he argued. "Moonlighting, or whatever they call it."

"No, I can't. I have a conflict of interest."

"That doesn't bother me."

"Well, it bothers me," she snapped. Her gaze flicked to his

face. He didn't know what she saw there, but her own expression suddenly softened. "Look, I'm sorry, but...no."

No.

Simon sat on the corner of his desk. Well, that was clear. Confronted by a million unanswered questions, he'd pushed her for a response, and he'd gotten one.

Too bad it wasn't the one he wanted.

He continued to stare at her, trying to figure out what he could possibly say or do to change her mind, to persuade her to help him, to stay with him, to be with him.

He closed his eyes, dizzy with the force of his need.

She cleared her throat. "How's your head?"

"What? Oh." He reached up to touch the swelling above his ear. "It hurts."

"Have you had it looked at yet?" she asked.

As if, he thought wryly, now that she had slapped him down, she was trying to soften the blow.

"No."

She took a step closer. His body went on alert. "Maybe you should," she said.

His mind snapped into action, testing, weighing options.

He angled his head. "Be my guest."

She took another step forward.

Cautious, he thought. But not a coward.

Her hip, in navy blue polyester, brushed his thigh. She raised her hand; hesitated. And then, very gently, threaded her fingers through his hair.

She smelled like sun and water, like shampoo and...gasoline? For a second he thought his mind might be playing tricks on him again, and then he remembered her boat.

"It looks bad," she said.

"It's clean."

"Tough guy." His scalp tingled as her touch feathered through his hair. "You should have had stitches."

"Too late now."

"Yeah." She started to draw away.

He grabbed her wrist.

"Hey," she protested. "You've already got one bump on the head. Don't make me hurt you again." But her pulse thrummed under his thumb.

Simon's grip tightened. Maybe he'd pushed for the wrong response before. Maybe he'd asked the wrong question.

At least he could settle one damn thing.

Leaning forward, he covered her mouth with his.

Chapter 3

If Laura had let herself think about kissing Simon Ford ahead of time… Okay, so she had thought about it. Big deal. Anyway, she'd expected him to kiss the way he talked. Cool. Controlled. Kind of dry.

She missed the target all three times.

His kiss was hot, wet and deep. He kissed like he was starving for her, like he wanted everything, wanted her. And instead of getting offended or disgusted or afraid, she yanked him closer and kissed him back.

Tongues. Teeth. Heat.

Sensation kicked through her system like rapid fire on a pistol range, all flash and fire and recoil. She was blinded, deafened, her palms sweaty and her mind a blank. She was operating on instinct and body memory, living purely in and for the moment. Her knees buckled.

Simon made an encouraging sound deep in his throat and widened his stance against the desk.

Wow. Pow. Even better.

His body was lean and hard. It fit hers as if they'd been carved from the same piece of oak, every plane and curve lined up and matching. Her starved system sparked and exploded. Wrapping her arms around his neck, she fed and devoured him.

But when his hand slid from Laura's arm and sought the shape of her breast through the heavy Kevlar vest she wore, another instinct kicked in. Something older and more urgent than sex.

Self-preservation.

"You… I…" She couldn't form words.

"'We'?" Simon suggested, a hint of a smile in his voice. But she noticed with a pinch of satisfaction that his breathing was as ragged as hers.

She shook her head, struggling for coherence and control. Oh, God. Oh, God. She'd really screwed up. "I don't mix sex with the job."

There, a whole sentence.

He arched an eyebrow. "You don't work for me. You can't call this harassment."

She stepped back, tugging on the bottom of her vest. "How about assaulting an officer?"

His eyes narrowed. "Is that what you think this was?"

"No. Sorry." Her face flooded with heat. "I'm just… My brain's still on Planet Stupid."

"I'm feeling a little out of this world myself," he murmured.

It was geeky. And charming.

Laura scowled. "Yeah, well, it's time to come back to earth. This can't happen again."

"Why not?" he asked curiously.

"You're the genius. You figure it out."

"You're not giving me enough data to draw a conclusion."

"There are cops who mess around on the job, okay? It's like a crime of opportunity. You'd be surprised how many people out there are willing to make it with anything in a uniform. Heck, I've been propositioned by guys I had handcuffed in the back of the squad car."

He studied her with quiet intensity. "Did it work?"

She couldn't tell if he was joking or amazingly clueless. "I don't get involved on cases I'm investigating."

"You're not investigating my case."

He had her there.

"Doesn't matter," she said. "I don't get involved."

His brows raised. "Ever?"

"Not recently."

"Define recently."

She stuck out her jaw. This conversation was even more risky than sex. She didn't "do" intimacy. She couldn't afford it. "Are you asking for my sexual history, Ford?"

"I think now that we've swapped saliva you could share the highlights." His eyes gleamed. "You might even start calling me by my first name."

She didn't want to be amused, damn it. Or to share the messy details of her personal life. But maybe she could give him enough to shut him up. To shut him down.

"I was married," she said. "A long time ago."

"What's a long time? Two years? Five?"

He was a scientist. It figured he wanted answers, specific, quantifiable data. As if all the fear and pain she'd felt then could fit some tidy little chart.

"What does it matter?" she asked.

His gaze never left her face. "I like numbers," he said simply.

"Okay, fine. Ten."

He couldn't quite keep the surprise from his face. "Ten years. And…?"

"And what do you think?" Her shoulder jerked in an ill-tempered shrug. "I was eighteen. It didn't work out."

"What happened? He cheated on you, beat you, broke your heart?"

"He died."

As soon as the words were out of her mouth, she regretted them. She didn't mind being blunt. Hell, she took pride in it. But that had been a cheap shot, designed to shock. It was unworthy of her. Simon's kiss had rattled her more than she wanted to admit.

"I'm sorry," Simon said calmly.

"Don't be. The relationship was on life support even before Tommy died."

"What happened?"

Simon's voice was quiet, unthreatening, like a doctor's or a priest's. Laura was trained in interview techniques. She knew better than to fall for that nonjudgmental tone. But she responded to it anyway.

"Tom Baker was a seaman at the Great Lakes Naval Training Facility. I was a teenage girl in Chicago with more attitude than smarts. I got pregnant, we got married, he got killed two months later in some freak training accident. End of story."

"Not quite," Simon said.

"You mean the baby?" Her throat clogged with tears. Her fault. Her stupid fault, for letting a moment of sexual excitement crash her usually strong barriers. Damn, damn, damn.

"There was no baby," she said harshly. "I lost it a couple weeks later."

If he had reached out to touch her, she would have bolted. But he sat, unmoving—unmoved?—against his flat, polished desk, his light eyes focused on her face.

"You were very young," he observed.

"I was stupid."

His lips parted, as if he were about to say something, and then he stopped.

Not so comfortable when it isn't all about numbers, are you? Laura thought, not without sympathy.

But he surprised her.

"That must have been hard," he said.

"I…" She cleared her throat. "I got over it. I am over it."

"Good. Go out with me."

Her heart bumped, which annoyed her. "Haven't you heard a word I've said?"

"Yes," he answered promptly. "You're not my employee, you're not investigating my case, and you're not grieving for your late husband. So I see no barriers to our becoming involved."

None. Except her father had worked for the company contracted to provide his security, and the old man was missing now along with a cache of cultured rubies valued at half a million dollars. And this afternoon at the end of her shift, Laura was going to have to report that theft to her boss.

"Except I'm not interested," she said.

Simon didn't point out that her kiss had definitely been interested. Either he was actually a nice guy, or he was experienced enough to know better.

"Let me know if you change your mind," he said.

She shook her head, unreasonably tempted. "It would never work."

"Why not?"

"I'm not your type."

"How do you know?"

"Look at me," she said, her voice rising with frustration. "Look at *us*. You're Millionaire Inventor Guy, and I'm—"

"—an incredibly attractive woman with practical knowledge and principles."

A pleased flush swept over her. "Thanks."

But she knew who and what she was: a small-town cop with a troubling connection to his case. And those principles he was talking about wouldn't let her gloss over the differences between them.

She squared her shoulders. "But the answer's still no. Detective Palmer is handling the investigation from here on in. After today, there's no reason for us to ever see each other again."

He blew it.

Simon didn't know how or why, but he couldn't shake the feeling of connections missed, of opportunities lost. It was like calculating a complex equation. His formula was correct, but his data was wrong. Or he was missing a variable completely.

He watched the police boat's choppy progress across the lake, aware of Laura Baker's slim, straight figure at the controls. She'd taken off her hat, making her neatly constrained hair gleam like tarnished metal in the sun.

He inhaled sharply. He wanted her. Still. The taste of her lingered in his mouth like honey. The itch for her buzzed in his blood.

She wanted him, too. He might not remember whatever women had occupied his bed or his mind before, but he recognized a woman's desire.

But it didn't take a genius to see that this woman was equally determined not to have anything further to do with him.

Why not?

Considering the problem logically, there was nothing obviously wrong with him. Well, except for the void where his memory should be. And while the detective was smart enough to suspect the worst, she couldn't know the full extent of his loss.

No one could know the full extent of his loss.

Expelling his breath, Simon turned back to his desk. Laura Baker was a puzzle and a challenge. But however much he might enjoy fitting the pieces together, he had bigger problems to solve.

"I didn't mean to screw things up with the meter maid," Dylan volunteered over lunch. "But she's not your usual type, is she?"

Simon lowered his fork to stare at his brother, seated nine feet away at the opposite end of the long, polished table. All of the furniture in the house was over-sized and shiny, as if it had been designed for very neat giants. The colors were all neutrals, cream and beige and gray. Simon wondered if he'd chosen them or even liked them. He didn't like them now. Would he when he got his memory back?

"Detective," he corrected his brother. "And why isn't she my type?"

"Because she's difficult. And you've always liked your women easy."

Simon raised his eyebrows. "Easy?"

"No work," Dylan explained. "No hassles. The Stepford Girlfriends—beautiful, intelligent, perfect, polite. Like you could shut them off and put them away in the lab when you were done playing with them."

Simon was amused. Appalled. "I don't have a lot of time to invest in relationships," he said. *Now, where had that come from?*

Dylan snorted. "You're telling me. If you didn't have so much money, no woman would put up with you."

Could he ask about the portrait of the schoolgirl upstairs? Simon wondered. No, not yet.

"What about you?" he asked.

"Are you offering me a raise, big brother?"

"No." Should he? What did his brother earn?

"That's okay. I don't need more money." Dylan grabbed a roll from the basket in the center of the table and buttered it lavishly. "I have charm."

Quinn Brown stomped into the dining room. He glared at Dylan and shoved a phone handset at Simon.

No charm there, Simon thought.

"Call for you," Quinn said. "Vince Macon."

"Damn," Dylan said.

Who the hell was Vince Macon?

Simon had spent some time yesterday studying his company's organization chart, trying to grasp its structure, hoping to strike a name that would spark a memory. In the process, he'd learned that Lumen Corp employed over a hundred researchers and support staff at its Chicago headquarters and that his brother Dylan—surprise, surprise—was a vice president of marketing. But he didn't recognize the name "Macon" at all.

He had to say something. Do something.

"You take the call," he said to Dylan.

His brother's face froze. If Simon had been in the mood for a laugh, it would have been funny.

"You're kidding," Dylan said.

"No. Why?"

"Because he's one of your biggest investors and he hates me?"

An investor. Relief eased Simon's shoulders.

"Good enough," he said and accepted the phone. "Hey, Vince. Simon here."

"Simon!" The voice was hearty, warm…and completely unfamiliar. Simon squelched his disappointment. "You're a hard man to reach. What are you doing on the island?"

"Research," Simon said.

"Ha. Good one." Vince Macon lowered his voice. "I heard Dylan was up there with you."

Simon looked down the table. His brother had settled back in his chair and was watching him. "Yes."

"Do you think that's a good idea?"

"I don't know," Simon said honestly, meeting Dylan's eyes. "But he's here."

"You mean, in the room? Listening?"

"Yes."

"You're not having any…trouble up there, are you?"

A prickle of disquiet raised the hair on the back of Simon's neck. Trouble? Yeah. He had a bump on his head, a missing cache of cultured gemstones and great big gaps in his memory. But why would Macon ask? How would he know?

"No," Simon said finally. "No trouble."

"Good. I'll talk to you later then. When are you coming back to Chicago?"

Frustration bubbled inside him. He was stumbling around in a fog, trying to avoid dangers he could not see. His blindness was bad enough here, where the only people he bumped into were his brother and Quinn Brown. Who knew what problems would trip him up outside? Better perhaps, safer perhaps, if he stayed in safe isolation on the island until his memory returned.

But his mind remained a stubborn blank. Sometimes he had a flash, a moment's hope. Last night he'd reached for his nail clippers, and his pleasure at finding them in the drawer he'd opened so automatically had been embarrassingly acute.

He couldn't count on such moments. They were frustratingly rare in any case. His business, his life, even his own character were like a puzzle he had to assemble without all the pieces or any real idea of what the finished picture was supposed to look like.

And yet his business and his life might depend on his ability to fit it all together.

Every day that slipped away took with it another chance to compile the pieces and make sense of the puzzle. Who had attacked him? Who had betrayed him? Who could he trust?

"Simon? You still there?"

Simon collected himself. "Yes. I'll be back in the office soon. A day or two. I'm close to something here."

He wasn't close to anything, he thought bleakly.

Or anyone, apparently. The only person he felt a connection with had just told him flat out there was no reason for them to ever see each other again.

At least Laura had been honest with him.

"Great," Vince said. "I'll see you then."

They said a few more words and disconnected. Simon set the phone beside his plate.

Dylan leaned forward, stabbing his lettuce with a fork. "So what did the old bastard want?"

"What do you think he wanted?" Simon countered.

Dylan swallowed a mouthful of salad. "He probably told you to kick me out before I talked you into funding my foolish, evil schemes."

"I can't kick you out. You're my brother. And a vice president of the company," Simon added.

Dylan grimaced. "That's always been an afterthought for you, hasn't it?"

Had it? Simon wished again, desperately, he could ask for an explanation. He went fishing for one instead.

"You're still my brother."

"Half brother," Dylan said.

It was another puzzle piece. Simon seized on it. "We still grew up together."

Dylan gave him an odd look. "If that's the way you want to remember it."

Simon didn't remember his childhood at all. He had a sudden image of wedging himself on the floor between his bed and the wall to read, and a shelf full of books. But no house. No yard. No memory of friends. Not even an impression of his mother's face.

Why were there no pictures of his mother in the house? No family at all, except the girl upstairs.

He wanted to ask, but he was afraid to show any weakness.

Laura would have asked. No one would have counted it a weakness. No one would be suspicious if she was around asking questions. It was a function of her job, a component of her character.

Simon needed answers.

He wanted an ally.

He needed Laura.

He wanted Laura.

Chapter 4

The apartment door jerked open a crack, and Laura Baker scowled past the security chain at Simon.

He was so glad to see a familiar face—even half of a familiar face—he decided to overlook the scowl. The walk through town had been a nightmare. He kept imagining people were looking at him, that they knew him or at least knew of him, and he hadn't recognized a soul. Not the straw-haired waitress smoking in front of the diner or the man in the checkered shirt cleaning the windows of the hardware store or the redheaded woman waving through the window of the camera shop. It had been a relief to turn onto Laura's tree-lined, residential street and into the quiet courtyard of her brownstone apartment building.

"What are you doing here?" she demanded.

"I want to talk to you. Please," he added, because she didn't seem nearly as happy to see him as he was to see her, and he needed her help.

The door didn't budge. "How did you get here?"

"Quinn brought me. In the boat."

He could tell from Quinn's reaction that that had been a mistake. But by the time Simon realized he knew how to pilot the boat, it had been too late.

"Well, I didn't think you walked on water." Laura's smile erased the sting from her words. The security chain rattled. "How did you know where I live? I'm not listed in the phone book."

He shrugged. "My computer's working."

She didn't cite antihacking statutes at him or protest his invasion of her privacy. Instead she swung open the door. "As long as you're here, you might as well come in."

Relieved, he stepped inside the cramped and airless apartment. "Nice place," he said, even though it wasn't. The stingy light from overhead barely illuminated the scarred woodwork and worn carpet.

Laura shrugged. "It's a dump. But it's convenient. I wanted to be close to the station. And it's got good bones."

He looked at her, her narrow face and straight shoulders, the way she stood with her fingers tucked into her back pockets, and the knots that had been twisting tighter and tighter in his gut relaxed. "Yes."

Did she color faintly in the dim light?

"You want something to drink?" she asked, walking away from him into the living room.

Throws and bright pillows failed to disguise the shabby furniture. The plant hanging by the window needed water. An empty glass decorated the coffee table, and a pair of sneakers lay kicked off by the couch. But Laura's home was still warmer, or at least more personal, than his luxury mausoleum.

"No drink. Thanks," he said.

She pivoted, her hands still in her pockets. The angle of her arms thrust her breasts forward. "Why are you here?"

He looked her carefully in the eyes. "I need a favor."

Her expression shuttered. What would it take, how would it feel, to have her look at him with openness? With warmth? "Yeah, I figured," she said.

"You said you wouldn't work for me," he reminded her.

"That's right."

"And you don't want us to be involved—romantically involved," he clarified.

The tilt of her chin was a challenge. "So?"

He wanted her. He wanted her mind and her mouth and her attitude. Simon had rehearsed his reasons on the way over and decided to his satisfaction that they were rational, viable and persuasive. But faced with that chin, he stumbled.

"I told you I couldn't remember anything from the time of the attack."

She nodded. "Short-term retrograde amnesia." He must have revealed his surprise, because she smiled. "I can look things up on the Internet, too. You want to sit down?"

"Thank you." He waited politely for her to drop into a chair and then folded himself on her couch, trying not to feel like a psychiatric patient.

"You know, if your memory's coming back, you should talk to Detective Palmer," Laura said.

"My memory's not coming back."

"No?"

"No. In fact..." Could he afford to tell her? Could he afford not to? "There's a lot I don't remember."

"Define 'a lot.'"

He drew a deep breath. "Quite a lot."

Her eyes narrowed. "Was there a reason you decided to

track me down at my apartment on my day off? Or do you just like yanking my chain?"

"Are you always this direct?"

"Yes."

He smiled. "Good."

She didn't smile back. "Are you always this evasive?"

"I don't know," Simon said. His heart jackhammered in his chest. "Or maybe I should say… I don't remember."

Her eyes jerked to his. She held his gaze for a long, slow moment.

Her breath hissed in. "You don't. You don't remember…*anything?*"

She believed him.

Simon's mouth went dry with relief. Or terror.

"I know enough to function," he said stiffly. "I think in time—"

"What about people?" she interrupted. He was grateful she didn't take out her notebook. He would have felt even more like a psychiatric patient. "What about your brother? You introduced him."

"Did I?"

Her eyes widened. "*Quinn* announced him. And then he introduced himself."

Simon nodded. "God knows what I would have done if he'd walked in without warning."

"Wow." She slumped back. "I bet you're having a hard time."

She understood. For a second, he didn't feel quite so alone.

"Yes," he admitted. "That's why I need your help."

She shook her head. "No, you don't. I'm sorry, but you don't. You need a professional."

They'd been over this before.

"You mean a doctor," he said flatly.

A shrink.

"A doctor would be good," she agreed. "But actually, I was thinking more along the lines of a private investigator. Somebody attacked you. Not only can't you identify whoever it was, you can't identify the people around you who might have a motive. You need someone who can make inquiries within your company and investigate your personal life."

He was pleased she understood his requirements so precisely. "That's why I need you."

"You need a security firm that specializes in executive protection or industrial espionage or something. Not me."

"I have a security firm that specializes in all those things. And they failed to do their job."

"But if you confided in them… If you explained…"

He stood. "E.C.I.P. has over three hundred employees working for almost twenty corporations. How long do you think I could keep my memory loss a secret if I confided in them?"

"They're not amateurs. Nobody's going to send out a company memo saying you've lost your mind. Memory," she corrected, blushing.

Trust Laura to put his worst fear into words.

"Mind will do," he said wryly. "Technically, amnesia is brain damage."

"But you're still Mr. Wizard Genius Guy, right?"

"I don't know," he said. His recent answer to everything. "I have journals, detailed journals, but recent ones appear to be missing. I can grasp the process, but I'm wasting time retracing my steps. And that could set my company back by months."

"Don't you have other researchers working on the same projects? Do you really think you're that irreplaceable?"

God help him, he did. His house might be devoid of

family photos and childhood memorabilia, but there were enough clues to the scope and nature of his accomplishments to make him both profoundly proud and deeply uneasy. The past few days had taught him how much he had lost.

And how much he had left to lose.

He walked to the window, staring sightlessly out at the street. With his back to her, he said, "I dropped out of MIT when I was twenty. I took a stake from my father to finance my first foray into research, inventing a new technology that increases the amount of information that can be distributed via fiber optics. Before he died, when I was twenty-seven, I was already a multimillionaire. My stock started trading publicly five years ago and my company is currently one of the hottest tech properties on the market. I received a National Medal of Technology for my work on laser surgery. The Pentagon has expressed interest in a nonlethal phaser device we have in development. If we're going to accept a Department of Defense grant, we can't afford the slightest doubt about my company's security or my abilities."

"You remember all that?" She sounded impressed. Too bad it wasn't justified.

"No. I read about it on-line. From an ABC News special report and a profile in *Newsweek*."

A Google search had yielded 1,378 pages of sources citing his education, inventions, patents and awards—and not a single personal fact beyond his birthdate. He was profoundly alone.

Laura's eyes narrowed. "At least it wasn't your obituary."

He couldn't tell if she was joking. He had a feeling— based entirely on his recent interactions with Quinn and his brother—that not many people teased him.

"Not yet," he said.

She frowned. "People are going to suspect something if I start hanging around asking questions."

A flare of hope, of excitement, shot up inside him. She was going to do it. At least, she was considering it.

Simon turned from the window, careful to keep his face and voice neutral. "Not if we give them a plausible reason for your presence."

"What reason? I've been removed from your case."

There it was. The sixty-four thousand dollar question.

His pulse jumped, an annoying reminder he wasn't as much in control of himself or the situation as he'd like to be. "We could allow people to believe we have a relationship."

"A relationship."

She was back to repeating things. Simon refused to take that as a bad sign. "Yes."

"A personal relationship," she clarified.

"Yes."

"A *sexual* relationship."

Not good, he thought.

"That was the idea."

"Your idea. Not mine." She got jerkily to her feet. "I wouldn't even go out with you. Why would I agree to pretend to be your—your…"

"Companion," he supplied. "And of course you would be compensated."

Warning flags flew in her cheeks. "Do it for the money?"

"You wouldn't have to do 'it.' Unless of course you wanted to."

Mistake, he thought instantly. She was already suspicious of his motives. He had to reassure her. Persuade her. Not antagonize her further.

"Please," he said. "This isn't simply a matter of questioning company employees. I need someone who might reasonably be expected to have an interest in my personal life. I need a woman."

"You must know plenty of women."

"No one I can trust."

No one he could remember.

No one else he wanted.

He took a step closer, moving in on her carefully. He didn't want to spook her into saying no. The woman had scruples. Defenses. Pepper spray.

"It won't work." Her voice was breathless and distracted.

"What?" He was watching her mouth, distracted himself.

"I can't help you."

Another step. "Why not?"

Her hair wasn't really brown, he decided, but bronze and gold and copper and rust, the colors running together like liquid metal.

"Conflict of interest," she said.

"What conflict? You're not investigating me. You're not even on the case."

"For good reason."

Her tension filled the air like static electricity, raising the hair on the back of his neck. "What reason?"

She drew back her head and looked him straight in the eye. "The guard—the missing guard—the one who disappeared the same night as the rubies? He's my father."

Simon went as rigid as a fighter absorbing a blow.

No wonder, Laura thought bleakly. She'd just delivered a whammy.

He didn't crumple. But he did move back a step. "When did you find out?"

She curled her hands into fists to hide their trembling. "When you told me his name."

"Good to know," Simon said.

She was shaking with relief and anticlimax. In her experience, men did not respond to damaging personal revelations with calm acknowledgment.

"That's it? 'Good to know'?" Her mimicry was savage.

Simon raised his eyebrows. "It certainly helps explain why your chief removed you from the case."

"Yes, it does," she said flatly.

She didn't blame Jarek Denko one bit for yanking her from the investigation. She could accept his reasons. She could abide by his decision. But that didn't mean she had to like it. She couldn't shake the feeling that her chief ultimately hadn't trusted her to do her job. He'd placed a higher value on the appearance of propriety than his belief in her integrity. And it stung.

"Did he do it?" Simon asked.

She narrowed her eyes. "What?"

"Your father," Simon said patiently. "Do you think he emptied the safe?"

She didn't know what to think. But she felt, in her bones and her soul, that her father could not be guilty. "No. The man I remember was a hardheaded, ham-handed son of a bitch, but he wasn't a thief."

"Fine," Simon said.

"What do you mean, 'fine'?"

He shrugged. "If you're right, there's no conflict of interest."

"And if I'm wrong?" She couldn't believe they were even having this discussion. He should have stormed out by now.

"Would you protect him?"

"Protect my father?"

"Yes. If you found out he was guilty, would you cover up for him or turn him in?" His odd, light eyes were opaque. Laura didn't have a clue what he was thinking.

"I guess I'd try to talk him into turning himself in," she said slowly. "But I'd have to know. I want to know."

Simon nodded. "Then we want the same thing."

His brain was more rapid than hers. Or maybe, Laura thought with a flash of resentment, his mind was clearer because his emotions weren't involved.

"What's that?" she asked.

"The truth." He gave her a thin smile which made her heart beat faster for no reason at all. "We both want the facts. As long as you don't let your hypothesis stand in the way of our reaching a logical conclusion, there's no reason we can't work together."

"How can you trust me?" The words burst out of her. "Have you lied to me?"

"No, but—"

"No."

"But Dan—the detective assigned to the case—is operating on the assumption that my father did it."

"And you are operating on the assumption that he didn't."

"Pretty much."

"I can accept your assumption," Simon said slowly. "As long as you can accept the possibility of his guilt."

Everything inside her recoiled.

But Simon's offer was fair. More than fair. He trusted her to do the right thing. And that meant almost as much to her as the chance to clear the old man.

"You do have one advantage over Palmer in this case," Simon said.

"Because I knew my father?"

"That, of course," Simon agreed coolly. "But also because, as the woman in my life, people will talk to you. You have the inside track."

She was trapped. Tempted. Torn. "Nobody is going to believe that I'm the woman in your life."

"My brother already does."

"Your brother was trying to annoy you."

He didn't deny it.

Laura scowled. "Anyway, nobody else will."

Simon's austere face never changed expression. But there was a brief flash of—something—in his eyes that made her shiver. Triumph?

"Then we'll have to do our best to convince them." He bent his head.

Her heart pounded. He was going to kiss her again. Unless she jumped out of range, unless she said no, unless she told him firmly and flatly he was out of his mind and she had no intention of going along with his schemes, he was going to kiss her.

She didn't move.

"This is a really bad idea," she said.

Simon stopped, his mouth a whisper away. "It's a kiss. Just one kiss. To seal our bargain."

She hadn't agreed to any bargain. But one kiss… She swayed toward him. How big a deal could one kiss be?

His mouth brushed hers, softly, gently, warmly. He smelled delicious, like cool sheets and hot male, and he tasted even better. He pressed his lips to hers, still gently, still warmly, without urgency and with only a hint of tongue. And she realized, with an odd sense of abandoning herself to her fate, that one kiss wasn't going to be enough.

Angling her head, she stood on tiptoe to kiss him back. His hands, his arms, gathered her close. She wasn't wearing her vest this time, and she felt all of him against all of her, chest, stomach, thighs.

She melted. Just melted. Her bones dissolved, her brain turned to mush. All she could think was how amazingly good he felt, hot and hard against her. The heat of him set fire to her blood and blew her doubts and resolutions away like smoke.

She kissed him again, longer this time. Deeper. His hands slid down to cup her rear end. Her palms glided up the long, smooth muscles of his back. Her brain was in flames, her body on fire. She clutched at him, learning him with her fingers, the silk of his hair, the shape of his skull, the hot bump above his ear...

He flinched and hissed.

She jerked and pulled away. "Did I hurt you?"

His eyes were nearly black. "It doesn't matter." He reached for her again.

"Yes, it does."

Oh, God, what had she done? What was she doing?

She stepped back, crossing her arms over her chest, struggling for control. For distance.

"Okay." Her voice was shaky. "I guess we've established that an attraction between us is—isn't completely unbelievable."

Simon's gaze never left her face. "We've certainly convinced me," he murmured.

Blood flamed in her cheeks. She ignored it. "So you want me to pose as your—"

"Companion."

"—girlfriend, so I can investigate your case and help you hide your memory loss from your employees."

"As well as hiding your involvement from your boss."

Oh, help. She hadn't even thought of that.

"You understand I'm only doing this to clear my father."

"Understood."

"I don't want any money," she said.

He nodded slowly. "All right."

She shoved her hands in her pockets. "Okay."

"So we have a deal?" Simon asked.

"I... Yeah, sure. It's a deal."

His smile glinted. "Do you want to shake on it?"

Her pulse leapt. Her throat constricted.

Just one kiss. To seal our bargain.

"That's okay," she said hastily. "I trust you. Your word is good enough for me."

Simon laughed—the first time she had heard·him laugh.

And she wondered, with a sinking feeling in the pit of her stomach, if she was about to get a whole lot more than she'd bargained for.

Chapter 5

The morning was not going according to plan. Nothing was going according to plan.

Simon had intended to spend the hours in his lab. But Laura, instead of waiting on his orders and convenience, had shown up twenty minutes ago in a rented Sunfish she'd sailed herself and tied to his dock. The boat bobbed beside his hulking white cabin cruiser, looking sleek and serviceable and out of place.

Laura, her angular face pink from the sun, perched on a deck chair. "You need to have a party."

Simon appreciated her enthusiasm. He did. But there was no way in hell he was going to surround himself with strangers.

"I hate parties," he said.

She tossed her braid over her shoulder. "How would you know? You can't remember anything."

He stiffened. Was she mocking him? But her eyes were candid and bright, her smile without malice.

He smiled back cautiously.

How *did* he know he hated parties? He wracked his memory, but there was nothing, no record of social disaster or personal humiliation, only a faint antipathy and a brief, sharp image of lying on his bed, staring at the press-on stars on his ceiling while laughter and music floated up the stairs. *His father was getting married again.*

Simon blinked, and it was gone.

"Parties are a waste of time," he said.

"Well, this one won't be," Laura said certainly. "How else am I going to meet people and ask questions?"

He hadn't thought about it. "You could come with me to Chicago."

She snorted. "Oh, yeah, like that'll fly. I have to work, you know."

"So do I," Simon said, but she ignored him.

"I have the Tuesday-Friday shift this week. So we could plan the party for this weekend. Saturday, maybe."

"Saturday is too late. I need to at least put in an appearance at the office. My investors are already wondering where I am."

"And when you can't find your own office, what will they think?"

Frustration welled inside him. He struggled to contain it before it spilled over and swamped them both.

"I'll figure it out," he said. He wasn't stupid. "I need to do something. The longer I'm out of the equation, the less I can control the results."

"So your showing up at the office is a deterrent?"

He nodded. "Or a catalyst."

"It's a risk," she warned.

"That's why I want you to come with me."

"And do what? I can't wander around the building introducing myself as your girlfriend and expect everybody you work with to tell me how they really feel about you and what they were doing last Wednesday night."

Put that way, she certainly had a point. Damn it.

He'd asked for her help. He'd wanted her insight and experience. Was he really going to risk losing her because he didn't want to give up control?

"Why a party?" he asked.

Laura leaned forward eagerly. "People talk at parties. It's a chance to bring together a specially chosen group of people and—and observe them in a controlled environment."

"Like lab rats," Simon said dryly.

She grinned, not offended at all by his analogy. Or was she amused he'd caught her attempt to speak his language? "Yeah. You should love it."

She was funny. He liked her teasing, her directness, her refusal to be intimidated by his intelligence and position. Would he have liked her before his bump on the head?

"How do we decide who to invite?" he asked.

"Ask Quinn to draw up a guest list. You can tell him I've been bugging you to meet the significant people in your life, and you don't want to be bothered right now."

Simon grimaced.

"What's the matter?" Laura asked.

"You think I'd do that?"

"Do what?" She was genuinely confused.

"Make you organize your own meet-my-friends-and-family party. Don't you think that's kind of…" He hesitated.

"Practical?" she suggested.

"Cold," he decided. "It's cold."

She shrugged. "You don't exactly have a reputation as

Mr. Warmth, you know. Anyway, what does it matter? It's all a cover to make the right people available for questioning."

She was right. He knew she was right. He still didn't like it.

She touched him, her fingers warm and light on his arm. "Are you worried about your safety? Because there's a good chance whoever was behind the attack will be present."

"Return to the scene of the crime?"

"Yes."

"Good. If I'm no use as a catalyst, maybe I can be rat bait."

She scowled. "That's not funny. The person who slugged you could be standing right next to you and you wouldn't know it."

The same thought had occurred to him. But he said, "Isn't that the idea? To see how people act and react around me?"

"React, yes. Attack you, no."

He shrugged. "So I'll be careful."

"And stay close to me," she ordered.

She was sitting on the edge of the deck chair, dressed in straight dark jeans and a plain white T-shirt that clung to her torso in the heat. There was nothing overtly sexual about her pose, her clothes or her suggestion. But just looking at her made his blood heat.

How close did she have in mind? Side by side? Body to body? Skin to skin?

"Yo, Ford." She was squinting at him, her brown eyes narrow with suspicion or annoyance. "Are you with me?"

"All the way," Simon said.

"Let E.C.I.P. know you want to lay on extra security for the party. Bodyguards."

He was still distracted by the image of Laura, up-close and preferably naked. "A bodyguard didn't help me the last time."

She winced, and he remembered, too late, that the bodyguard in question was her father. *Way to go, genius.*

He struggled to recover. "Have you talked with him yet?"

"My father? No."

"He's still missing?"

"Yeah."

He searched for something appropriate to say. "Well, you can talk to him when he gets back."

"Maybe."

This was not going well. Simon studied Laura's averted face, trying to recall what she'd told him about her father. *The man I remember was a hardheaded, ham-handed son of a bitch, but he wasn't a thief.*

Was. Wasn't. Past tense.

Simon lost his breath. Inhaled carefully. "Do you think he's dead?"

Her mouth dropped open. She snapped it closed. "Dead? No."

Okay, wrong question. He had no idea how to engage a woman in a discussion of her personal life. He couldn't remember ever wanting to before. Hell, he couldn't remember anything. But he did know that when one hypothesis failed, you tried another.

"So what's the problem? Why won't you speak with him?"

She turned to the water, for once not meeting his eyes. The wind flung bits of hair around her face, obscuring her expression. "I should have said he won't talk to me."

He was missing something. Some fact, some variable, that would make sense of her words.

"Fine. Why won't your father talk to you?"

"Because he still hasn't forgiven me for getting knocked up in high school." She turned to look at him then, her face faintly flushed and perfectly composed. "He hasn't talked to me in ten years."

Simon still didn't get it. He had his missing data; he just

couldn't make it fit the equation. He tried to picture Laura, pregnant at seventeen, trying to find her way between an unforgiving father and an irresponsible lover. But the image didn't compute with the cool-eyed, competent detective sitting in front of him.

I got over it. I am over it.

Maybe, he thought.

"So even after ten years, you still think you know him well enough to rule him out as a suspect?"

Her chin stuck out. "Yes. Pete Swirsky doesn't accept mistakes or excuses. Everything is right or wrong with him. Black or white. If he was angry enough, he might have hit you. But he'd never have robbed you."

Simon's blood ran cold with possibility and then hot with anger.

"Did he ever hit you?"

Her shoulder jerked. "What does that have to do with anything?"

It didn't. But it mattered to him. She mattered.

The awareness sat oddly on him, like a suit jacket that didn't quite fit. But he couldn't shrug it off.

He made an effort to speak evenly. "I'm trying to figure out why you're so eager to defend him."

The chin went up another notch. "I don't like to see the department make a mistake. And whatever is between us, the guy is still my father."

"Too bad he doesn't feel the same way."

"I don't care what he feels," Laura said flatly. "I do my job."

Simon thought she cared more than she let on. But maybe her stubborn faith in her father was the ultimate payback for his lack of faith in her.

"That's all anyone can ask of you," Simon said.

"Yeah, well, speaking of which…" She got to her feet, brushing her hands on the thighs of her jeans. Nervous? Or dismissive? He didn't know her well enough to tell. "I should get back to it."

He was surprisingly reluctant to see her go. "Don't you have the day off?"

"Monday, yeah. But—"

"Stay for lunch."

She looked almost flustered. "I don't want to be a bother."

"It's no bother," he assured her. "Quinn does the cooking."

Her hands stilled. Her head came back up. "That's what I meant. I don't want to be a bother to your butler."

"You need to talk to him about that guest list," Simon said.

"Right. But—"

"If we're going to convince him we're romantically involved, he's going to have to see us doing something more than argue on the deck," Simon said smoothly.

"Maybe we could sell tickets," Laura grumbled. But she sat back down.

It was a small concession. But he was unaccountably pleased by it.

He pressed the intercom button he'd discovered by the tall French doors. "Two for lunch, Quinn."

"Where's your brother?" Laura asked.

"He returned to Chicago this morning."

It had been a relief to be rid of Dylan's sharp eyes and barbed conversation. But the big house felt even emptier after he'd gone.

Laura stood again and prowled restlessly to the railing. Simon stayed where he was, admiring the way she moved.

"Are you sure there's enough food?"

"Quinn will take care of it."

She snorted.

"He does his job, too," Simon said mildly. "But if you're concerned—or very hungry—I can send him into town to restock the refrigerator."

"You don't shop in town," she said. "You haul all your supplies in from Chicago."

He filed the fact away, one more idiosyncrasy to be learned and dealt with. "Is that a problem?"

She straightened from the rail, her clear brown eyes gauging the seriousness of his question. "It can be. Some of the local merchants really feel the pinch in the off season. It doesn't help when the town's wealthiest resident buys his groceries someplace else."

"I didn't know," Simon said.

Or hadn't cared.

He didn't much like that possibility, but he was still a scientist. He couldn't pick and choose his data to support whatever theory of himself he wanted.

"Well, now you do," Laura said lightly. "Can we eat? I'm starved."

They went into the long, polished dining room. The first thing Laura did was grab her place setting and slide it closer to Simon's. The table immediately shrank to more human proportions. Why hadn't he thought of doing that when Dylan was here?

"Man, this is great," she said after Quinn had served them. Thin slices of cold smoked salmon rested on a bed of greens decorated with finely chopped egg and onion, crisp curls of butter and triangles of bread. "No wonder you don't cook."

"I can cook," Simon said, surprising them both. He saw strips of red and yellow peppers against a scrubbed chopping block, and the wide silver knife in his own hand. It wasn't much. Barely a memory. But his heart pounded.

To quiet it, he said, "I just don't take the time usually. What about you?"

"Same thing. No time and nobody to appreciate it." Laura stopped piling lox on rye long enough to grin at him with that sharp, disarming honesty he admired. "Plus, I'm a lousy cook."

"With a name like Baker?"

Her laugh slipped out. "Yeah. It doesn't seem right, does it? But there was never anybody around to teach me. You?"

"I…" He fished for another image, a memory, but there was nothing. Frustration tightened his mouth.

"It's all right," she said quietly. "It'll come eventually."

"Maybe it won't." There was a hollow inside him, keener than hunger. "Maybe I don't remember anyone because there's no one to remember. Cooking is all measurements and formulas anyway. I probably taught myself from books."

Saying it made it feel real. Feel right. He could almost be that boy beside the bed, wedged where no one could see him, his back to the cool plaster and a book on his knee.

Simon? Simon, come down and meet your new mother.

"Simon?" Disoriented, he looked down at Laura's hand on his forearm and then up into her concerned eyes. "You okay?"

"Fine."

He wasn't fine. He felt dizzy, suspended between Simon past and Simon present, swinging between the needy, lonely boy he'd been and the self-sufficient scientist he'd become. Only Laura's hand on his arm anchored him.

Quinn came in with a plate of fruit and cookies and went out again.

Simon waited until he'd gone and then said, "You should bring some stuff over."

Laura removed her hand to reach for a cookie. He missed her touch. "What kind of stuff?"

"Clothes. A toothbrush. Stuff," he repeated. What did he know about what a woman needed? "To convince people we're actually involved."

"You really think Quinn is poking through your closet and medicine cabinet for clues to your love life?"

He had no idea. It was obvious he'd chosen to live his life uncluttered. Unencumbered. But he found he liked the thought of Laura's things in his house.

"It's possible," he said stiffly.

Laura bit into a cookie. Chocolate. It left a tiny smear at the corner of her mouth. "Okay."

He watched her tongue chase that elusive taste of chocolate, wishing he could lick it off for her. "Okay, what?"

"Okay, I'll bring a few things over. Do you like stuffed animals?"

"Stuffed…" He dragged his gaze from her mouth to meet her eyes, bright with laughter. She was teasing him.

He exhaled in relief. "Sure."

"Perk the place up," she offered, straight-faced.

"It is a little—"

"Cold? Boring? Sterile?"

"—impersonal in here," he admitted.

Laura glanced around his beige-on-beige decor, all blank walls and clean, bare surfaces, without even the splash of color that hung over the fireplace. "Pictures would help."

"Fine. Bring me a picture."

Hold on. Just because she'd agreed to the girlfriend thing didn't mean she would roll over for him. "I'm not your personal shopper, Ford. Buy your own artwork."

"No, a real picture," he said impatiently, like he was a shift commander and she was a not-very-bright patrolman. "Of you. For my office."

Oh.

Laura nibbled her lip. Should she be flattered? Or should she chalk his request up to that amazing consider-all-options, cover-all-bases mind?

"You don't seem like the kind of guy who keeps a picture of his girlfriend on his desk."

"That's what would make it so convincing."

Maybe.

"Okay," she agreed. "As long as you don't already have another woman stashed away somewhere in a silver frame…"

His expression shifted. His eyes shuttered.

Ha, she thought. Gotcha. But under the satisfaction she felt something very close to a pang.

"What did you just remember? Ex-wife? Girlfriend?"

"No, nothing like that."

"But something," she guessed.

"One picture," he snapped. "Upstairs. Do you want to see it?"

"Is this like, 'come look at my etchings'?" But she pushed away from the table and followed him up the stairs.

This time, instead of turning right toward his office, they turned left. Two doors interrupted the flow of this corridor: a linen closet and, there on the end, the master suite.

During her earlier search of the house, Laura had barely been in the room long enough to notice the hardwood floors, the charcoal gray walls, the king-size bed under the supersize skylight. Okay, so she hadn't missed that bed. She wasn't blind.

But she hadn't paid attention to the photograph on his dresser. Her mistake. Shoving her hands in her pockets, she studied it now, aware of Simon brooding beside her.

The subject was white, female, mid to late teens. With makeup it was hard to say for sure. She had the soft cheeks of childhood, a mouth inclined toward sulking and Simon's eyes. Her hair, dyed blond, was chopped at chin-length, and a row of tiny silver hoops decorated one ear. Laura counted them. Eight.

"Who is she?"

"I don't know."

And it bothered him. She could see how much in the set of his shoulders, the rigid line of his mouth.

"I could find out for you," she said.

"How?"

"Tax records. Birth records. Driver's license, maybe. She looks old enough to have one."

"Do you have time for that?"

Not really. "I have the rest of the afternoon."

He shook his head. "It's not enough."

She wanted to help him. "I could get lucky. Although a search will take longer if she doesn't have your name."

She didn't point out how much the girl resembled him. He could see that for himself.

His face was set as stone.

Gently, Laura said, "If she's out there, I'll find her."

"Finding her is not your top priority," he said stiffly.

His I-am-a-rock routine was pissing her off. She wasn't looking to take on his problems. She had plenty of her own. But he'd asked for her help, hadn't he? And she was drawn to respond by some reluctant recognition of soul, by a need more compelling than attraction, more dangerous than sex. "If locating somebody who looks enough like you to be your daughter is not a top priority, what is?" she asked.

Simon drew himself up. "I appreciate your suggestions. But it's not my family you should be searching for. It's yours."

Chapter 6

By the time Laura drove up to the gates of Lumen Corp Technologies industrial park, she was hyped up and anxious and in a seriously bad mood.

Her fault, for ordering the triple venti mocha latte on the drive down from Eden.

Her fault, for pulling strings and calling in favors to get the afternoon off, and then wasting hours on lost opportunities and missed connections.

Simon's fault, for making her feel the whole damn trip was necessary.

The uniformed guard at the gate leaned through her car window. "Ms. Baker? Laura Baker?"

Not "detective," Laura noted. Simon obviously didn't want to advertise her police connection.

She hadn't spoken to him in two days. But despite that, despite the fact that she'd stalked off from lunch on Monday in tight-lipped silence, he'd still given her name to his security people. He still took her cooperation for granted. Bastard.

Or maybe he trusted her to do her job.

She handed the guard her ID, choosing her driver's license instead of the leather holder with her police identification.

He studied it, studied her, before handing back her wallet. Laura flushed. She'd accepted this gig. Resigned herself to it. But she felt naked without her shield, and she hated all this pretend girlfriend stuff.

She scowled. Something to remember next time she was tempted to lock lips with Simon Ford.

"Very good, Ms. Baker," the guard said. "Here's your parking pass. Visitors' lot is on the right. Someone will be there to meet you."

"Thanks."

She clipped the pass to her rearview mirror. As she drove away, she spotted a second security camera mounted on the outside of the gate house, recording her license plate number.

A smooth black ribbon of road wound through an immaculately tended landscape edged with bike paths and crossed with trails. The industrial park was twenty miles south west of downtown, between Midway Airport and the Argonne National Lab. Laura's lip curled in a purely defensive sneer. Simon probably paid more in property taxes than she made in a year.

The road curved around a stand of trees and emptied into two parking lots. And Laura's sneer dissolved in amazement.

Simon's headquarters were built into the side of a hill. One long outer wall of glass rose like a cliff from a reflecting pool, its double row of windows glinting like precious metal in the afternoon sun. Even the standard corporate landmarks—a flag, a sign, the massive glass-and-steel entrance—couldn't detract from the power and imagination of the place.

Laura parked her car, feeling as though she'd tumbled into some high tech fairy tale. Alice down the rabbit hole, maybe. The king under the hill. She reached into the back seat for her brown leather jacket and shrugged into it, adjusting it to cover the holster on her hip.

Her guide was waiting on the flagstone walk. Only instead of a white rabbit or a surly dwarf, her escort was a steel-haired woman in a red power suit and an ID badge on a silver cord.

Laura whistled silently. Even if she'd reviewed the dress code before she drove out here, she didn't have anything in her closet that fit these guidelines.

The woman smiled. Her lipstick was the exact same shade as her suit and her shoes. "Ms. Baker?"

Laura jammed her hands into her jacket pockets. "That's me."

"You'll need this." The woman handed Laura a bright yellow visitor's badge with the Lumen Corp logo in the background.

Laura studied it before slipping it over her head. "Quite a security system you've got here."

"Yes."

"Will this let me go anywhere in the building?"

"Only in the public areas."

"Right. So if I wanted, like, a tour, I'd have to…"

"You would need to be accompanied by an employee with the appropriate identification and coded passcard. This way, please."

Laura sighed. She hadn't really expected to hear anything different. One of the reasons her father looked guilty was that the lab could only be breached by someone with an appropriate passcard. She had requested a copy of the lab's computer access log and a list of people who had been issued the magnetic passcards from the security company. But since Denko had taken her off the case, that list had gone to Palmer.

Her guide moved briskly through the smoked glass doors. Laura followed, trying not to gawk. This soaring, sunlit entrance was a far cry from the Eden Police Department's shabby veneer-and-linoleum lobby.

A guard loomed on her left. Instinctively she stepped back and bumped into another guard on her right. One old, one young, both massive in matching black uniforms. Tweedledee and Tweedledum.

"Step this way, please."

She planted her feet. "What's going on?"

Tweedledee grabbed her arm. She considered jabbing her elbow into his gut and slamming her boot down on his instep; decided against it. He was just doing his job. And she was...

Ouch. She winced as he tightened his grip. She was getting mauled in the process.

"This way," he insisted.

Ms. Power Suit looked distressed, the first flicker of real feeling Laura had seen on her face. "Ms. Baker is Mr. Ford's personal guest."

"Yeah? Well, Mr. Ford's personal guest just set off the metal detector," Tweedledee—the older guard—said grimly.

"Take off your jacket, please," Tweedledum said from her other side. Laura glanced at his name tag. Dwayne something.

"You're new here, aren't you?" Laura's guide asked. "Mr. Ford is not going to be pleased that his guest was inconvenienced."

"Mr. Ford isn't going to be happy if his guest is packing heat, either."

Damn. They were attracting attention from all the shiny young people behind the desk. Laura could just imagine their reactions when rent-a-cop here discovered the sub compact Glock at her hip.

"Let's go someplace private. Dwayne," she suggested. "And we can—"

He brushed against her, too close for comfort. Too close, period. He swore. "She's armed."

The older guard spun her into the glass wall. The impact jarred her, shoulder, hip and thigh. Power Suit gave a distressed little cry as the guard grabbed Laura's forearms and wrenched her arms over her head.

She forced herself not to react, not to resist, to keep her muscles loose and her hands in sight. She knew guys like this. Guys like her father. They wanted a threat. Wanted a fight. They were itching for her to mess up, so they could prove what big badasses they were.

One of them snatched the gun from her belt. She hoped to God they didn't start waving it around. The G26 was one of the safest pistols designed, but you had to keep your finger off the trigger unless you intended to shoot.

"Police," she said as evenly as she could. "Identification—"

Hands fumbled at her waist, patted her sides, her breasts, her thighs.

She gritted her teeth. "Identification in my left back pocket."

They dug for it.

"You can't bring a gun in here," one of them said.

Yeah, she was getting that.

"I'm authorized to carry concealed," she said evenly. "I'm a—" Should she say detective? No, it would really chafe their butts to know she outranked them. Better if they assumed she was a patrol officer. "I'm with the Eden Police Department."

Her captor grunted. "Never heard of it." But he let up on her wrists.

Laura turned around and held out her hand for her ID.

He studied it one more time and then flipped it to her. She caught it one-handed.

Tweedledum—Dwayne—looked her up and down. "Sorry about the search."

Sure he was.

"Sorry about the gun." She extended her hand again. "I'll take it back now."

He hesitated.

"Mr. Ford is waiting," said the woman in the red suit.

Reluctantly he surrendered the Glock. Laura slipped it into its holster and adjusted her jacket.

He bared his teeth at her, not quite a smirk, not quite a sneer.

Something clicked. A memory. An impression. Keeping her face neutral, she asked, "Either of you know Pete Swirsky?"

Tweedledee's face scrunched. "Pete?"

"Swirsky?" asked Dwayne. "Sure. What's he up to?"

Laura's heart hammered. "I was hoping you could tell me."

He shook his head. "Nope."

"He's on vacation," the older man said. "Isn't that what you told me, he was on vacation?"

"Yeah. Vacation."

"When's he supposed to be back?" Laura asked.

The two men exchanged glances.

"What's this about?" Tweedledum asked.

Laura forced herself not to push. She wasn't prepared to conduct an interview. And while a good detective usually tried to break the ice at the start of an interview, getting felt up by your subject probably wasn't the best way to launch question-and-answer time.

She could get the answers she wanted later, from the security company's office. Or if they wouldn't speak with her, now that she was off the case, Simon could.

"Nothing. I just wondered if you knew him. Since you all work here."

"Mr. Ford is *waiting*," Ms. Power Suit repeated, an edge to her voice.

The guards shuffled their feet.

"Sure," Laura said. "Can't keep the boss waiting. Sorry."

She followed her guide across the marble floors, past massed green plants and trees in pots. It was like the lobby of some upscale, downtown hotel, complete with a massive counter at one end manned by twentysomethings with toothpaste-ad smiles and navy blue blazers.

Phones rang. Red heels tapped. The air smelled of flowers. Laura's guide stopped by a pair of recessed steel doors and scanned the back of her coded ID badge over a dark panel in the wall. The doors slid silently open. Impressive. It was going to be tough proving a flaw in the system.

"Does this go down to the Bat Cave?" Laura asked.

The woman's face didn't even twitch. "Mr. Ford's office is on the second floor. He's waiting for you."

Okay, so Simon had hired the woman for her efficiency. It sure as hell wasn't for her sense of humor.

They rode up in silence. The doors slid open on more plants, more marble, a grouping of leather chairs. Another shiny young person occupied a slightly smaller desk guarding another set of doors.

"Thank you, Andrew," Red Power Suit said, clearly dismissing him. She picked up the handset on the desk. "Mr. Ford, Ms. Baker is here. You can go in now," she said to Laura.

The young man, Andrew, jumped to open the door. She didn't notice him close it behind her.

Wowzers.

Simon's office was big—Trump-size—and furnished in ebony, charcoal and gray. Black leather chairs, crystal bowls, light fixtures that looked like they'd been grown out of rock or stolen from some museum of modern art. There was a sixty-two-inch plasma screen mounted on one wall, and enough computer equipment ranged around the room to upgrade the entire Eden Police Department. And the town library. Tall, tinted windows admitted the light and looked out on the park and reflecting pool.

Laura curled her hands into fists. She'd seen Simon's home before. She knew he was rich. But here, in the heart of his business operations, she saw more than wealth. She saw genius and ambition, discipline and drive.

What had it taken to build his empire? And what would he do to keep it?

He stood and came around his desk, backlit by the brilliant windows. And her heart stuttered helplessly.

Stupid. She couldn't help but be impressed. She didn't have to be intimidated.

She squared her shoulders and touched her elbow to her gun. "I see you found your office."

Simon stopped, warned by something in her voice. "So did you." He eyed her warily. When his assistant Carolyn had told him she was at the gate, he'd been glad. Grateful. Relieved. But now… "Why did you?"

"You told me to come."

Yes, he had. Before he'd offended her with his ill-judged crack about her father.

"You told me you were busy," he said.

"I am. I had to come into town anyway. The other end of

town." She prowled his office, her hands in her pockets, her quick gaze taking in everything.

Something was wrong, Simon thought. Maybe he wasn't wise in the ways of women, but even an idiot could see the agitation seething beneath her cool surface.

Of course, where Laura was concerned, maybe he was an idiot, Simon thought ruefully. But something had happened to upset her.

"We're a little south of your jurisdiction, aren't we?" he asked mildly. "Or does the Chicago Police Department depend on Eden for backup?"

She snorted. "That'll be the day." She stopped pacing to face him, hands jammed in her pockets. "I did what you wanted. I went to look for him. My father."

She hurled the words like stones. But Simon recognized both her concession and her courage in making it.

"Did you find him?" he asked.

"Not the first place I looked. He'd moved," Laura explained when Simon raised his eyebrows. "Son of a bitch moved from our old house without leaving a forwarding address."

And without telling his daughter.

He hasn't talked to me in ten years.

Son of a bitch, indeed.

"Then how did you find him?"

"I haven't yet. But I ran his license, got his new address."

"I could have gotten his address for you."

"I know. But maybe I didn't want to give you the satisfaction of knowing I was looking." She shrugged. "And maybe I hoped I could surprise you—locate my father, clear his name and solve the case, all on my afternoon off."

Her self-deprecating humor slid into him like a knife, pointed. Painful.

"Sounds like a plan."

"Oh, yeah. A great plan. Only none of his neighbors have seen him since the night you were attacked. Of course, I didn't talk to them all. Most of them were still at work."

"Did you go inside the apartment?"

She rolled a look at him, amused and disparaging. "How? The old man's been in the security business longer than I've been alive. He doesn't leave a spare key under the mat."

"You don't need a key. You're a police officer." And the old man's daughter, Simon thought, but now didn't seem the time to press it.

"I'm not on the clock. I'm not on this case." Laura turned away, started pacing again like a cat in a cage. Graceful. Annoyed. "Anyway, I'd need a search warrant."

"Not necessarily. There are other ways to get in."

"Breaking and entering?" She shook her head. "No, thanks."

"I could go with you." He wanted to be with her.

"Right. And then we could both get arrested. Maybe they'd give us adjoining cells."

He wasn't used to having his ideas dismissed, he discovered. It was a novel feeling. And not a pleasant one.

"I meant, I could go with you when you go back to talk to the neighbors."

"You'd do that?"

"Why not?"

He'd succeeded in surprising her. But she recovered quickly. "I don't need my hand held, Ford."

"I intend to do a lot more than hold your hand," he said coolly. "Get used to it."

She narrowed her eyes. "That bump on the head obviously didn't damage your ego."

"My ego is taking enough of a beating from you."

"Well, there's one problem I can solve for you." She strode toward the door. "I'm leaving."

He put out a hand to stop her. "Don't go."

His fingers closed around her wrist. She hissed. But she didn't hit him. He supposed he should be grateful for that.

"What's the matter?" he asked.

"Let go of my arm."

"Tell me what's wrong."

"Listen, I've been jerked around enough today," she said through her teeth. "Let go of my arm."

Jerked around…?

He studied her face, her eyes bright with temper, her mouth tight with annoyance. Or pain? Shifting his grip, he pushed her jacket sleeve out of the way to look at her arm. And swore.

A line of red blots decorated her arm, the first sign of bruising, the marks of someone's fingers.

"What's this?"

She pulled her arm away and tugged her cuff to cover the ugly red marks. "It's nothing."

"It doesn't look like nothing. Who the hell did this?"

"The Brute Squad."

He frowned at her, uncomprehending.

She sighed. "Security. Downstairs."

His reaction was instinctive. Immediate. Savage. Someone had hurt her. "I'll fire them."

Her mouth dropped open. "You can't do that."

"Watch me." He strode to the desk to pick up the phone.

She followed him. "They were just doing their jobs."

"Not here. Not any longer. Carolyn, get E.C.I.P. on the—"

Laura reached across him and smacked her hand on the phone, cutting him off. "Your security responded appropriately to a perceived threat. Simon, I'm armed. My gun set off the metal detector in the lobby."

"So they manhandled you."

"Well, they had to do something. They can't let people walk into the building waving weapons."

"You were waving your gun?"

"No. But—"

"Did they search you? Touch you?"

"They *disarmed* me."

And left welts in the process. He reached for the phone again. "They're gone."

"For heaven's sake, Simon, you can't fire people for protecting you. Especially now, when you need all the protection you can get."

"That's beside the point."

"No, that is the point. You were attacked in your own home. You need your security personnel."

"Not if I can't trust them," he snapped.

Wrong answer.

Color flooded her golden skin. Simon cursed himself silently. Way to go, smart guy. The only thing he seemed to have a genius for was putting his foot in his mouth.

"I wasn't referring to your father."

She glared at him. "Don't patronize me, Ford."

"All right." He drew a deep breath. "I wasn't referring *only* to your father."

She nodded shortly, accepting both his implicit apology and the truth. And then turned directly to the subject at hand. "Who else don't you trust?"

God, she was amazing. He wanted to kiss her.

"Pretty much everybody," he admitted. "Being here at the office is tougher than I thought."

"Is your memory coming back at all?"

"Not really. I've kept most of my appointments. It helps to meet people one on one, to be able to put names with faces."

"But what do you talk about?"

He shrugged. "I ask Carolyn to bring me the relevant files before each appointment."

Laura grinned. "Smart."

"Desperate," he corrected. But his mouth curved in an answering smile. "They seem to want to do most of the talking anyway. I've been concentrating on sitting back and looking noncommittal."

"So you're functioning," she said with approval.

"To a degree. I'm making more notes than decisions."

"That's okay. You can learn a lot by listening."

"Yes. In fact—" He stopped. It was stupid.

"In fact…" she prompted.

"I get the impression I'm not usually perceived as a good listener," he confessed.

Actually, it was more than that. Worse than that. All day long he'd been aware of conversations stifled in his hearing, of subordinates stiffening when he asked for their opinions. His assistant Carolyn moved around him with the deliberate care of a demolitions expert. The young man in the outer office fidgeted every time Simon stuck his head out of his office.

The actual impression Simon received was that his employees perceived him as an autocratic, insensitive, impatient son of a bitch.

"No surprises there," Laura said.

"Do I seem…arrogant to you?"

"Some. But I meant more that you're used to being smarter than everyone around you." She shrugged. "Why should you listen to them?"

Her tone made it clear she didn't condemn him. He was amazingly grateful to her for that. He was struggling to understand himself. That she understood him, even a little, made him feel much less alone.

She shot him a narrow look. "That doesn't mean it would hurt you to accept other people's advice every now and then."

He controlled his smile. "Your advice, you mean."

"Well, yeah."

"I do," he assured her sincerely.

"Since when?"

He arched one eyebrow. "I'm following your recommendation to have a party this Saturday night."

"Really? Where's the guest list?"

He reached into his desk and handed it to her. "I'd like to review it with you."

She scanned the list quickly. "It's going to be hard to get this many people together on such short notice."

"Quinn's already made most of the calls. I assumed that would be easier for you, since you said you had to work between now and Friday."

Her lips curved. "I guess you do listen."

He liked talking to her, liked making her smile. So he added, "I also reviewed my tax returns for the past few years."

"Right. Like I would ever give you tax advice. We are so not in the same financial bracket."

"I wasn't looking at the tax tables."

"So, what were you…" Her eyes widened. "You were looking for the girl in the photograph."

He nodded. "I haven't found her yet, though. No dependents."

"What about child support, child tax credits?"

"No."

"Alimony payments?"

Was she only asking out of professional interest? Simon hoped not. "Nothing."

"That's disappointing," Laura said.

He regarded her with some exasperation. "On the contrary. I find it reassuring to know I don't have a child out there somewhere."

"Not one you're acknowledging, anyway."

He was stung. "You think I'd shirk responsibility? Abandon a child?"

She folded her arms. "It happens."

He studied her stubborn face and unhappy mouth, and awareness crashed on him like a wave. "Did it happen to you?" he asked gently.

"We're not talking about me." The chin came up. "Anyway, Tommy married me, didn't he? He supported us."

Big deal. Simon admired her loyalty to her dead husband, but any man who was a man would do the same. Wouldn't they? Wouldn't he?

The truth was, he didn't know.

"I've traced automatic transfers to various personal accounts," he said stiffly. "I haven't identified all of them yet. But—"

The door to his office opened, and a strange blonde sailed in like a swan, graceful, sleek and confident.

Carolyn darted in her wake, a ruffled duck defending her territory. "I'm sorry, Mr. Ford, she—"

"Honestly, Caro, it's not as though I need an introduction," the intruder said.

Very cool, Simon thought. Very beautiful. She wore her age—midthirties?—and her diamonds lightly.

Her amused gaze raked over Laura. "Although in this case I might. You would be…"

"Laura Baker." She kept her hands in her pockets.

"Interesting." The woman looked at Simon, clearly expecting him to introduce her. When he didn't, she shrugged and smiled. "I'm Mrs. Ford."

Chapter 7

Laura balled her fists in her pockets. She didn't believe for one second that these two had ever been married. Maybe she didn't want to believe it.

The woman standing in Simon's office wearing Armani and an amused expression was at least several years older than he was. Her body was aerobically toned, her hair expertly highlighted, her makeup flawless. She probably drank the blood of virgins to stay young.

I'm Mrs. Ford.

Laura glanced at Simon to see how he was taking the news.

"That will do, Carolyn. Thank you," he said. The door closed quietly behind his assistant. Simon's face was blank. Polite.

Shock, Laura decided. Nobody's manners were that good. Her quick surge of protective feeling surprised her.

The woman's eyes slid to Simon. "I take it you haven't told her about me."

He crossed his arms, managing to mask his probable panic with indifference. "What's to tell?"

Oh, good job, Laura thought.

The perfect mouth pouted. "Darling, you'll hurt my feelings. After all we've been to each other…"

Bitch.

Think. A good detective resisted jumping to conclusions. It was up to Laura to weigh the evidence, to consider the options, to review the facts.

Simon had no dependents listed on his tax records. Anyway, this Mrs. Ford was definitely not the type to waive alimony. She was too young to be his mother, too old to be Dylan's wife. Which left…

"Which stepmother are you?" Laura asked.

"Mia."

Ha. So she was right.

"Number four," Mia added. "Since Simon apparently hasn't brought you up to speed yet."

"What do you want?" Simon asked.

"Quinn told me you were having a party. Which I know you hate and can't imagine you're prepared for. So I stopped by to offer my services."

"Considerate of you," Simon said coolly.

Laura stuck out her chin. "Exactly what services are you offering?"

Mia smiled. Her teeth were very white. Caps, Laura thought. "Oh, help in creating the party environment—the decor and lighting, linen and china. Menu, of course. Music. Transportation. Media coverage." Her manicured hand conjured visions in the air. "Whatever Simon needs."

"We were thinking beer and brats in the backyard," Laura said.

The hand fluttered and came to rest on Mia's throat. "Simon?"

Simon's eyes gleamed. "She's pulling your leg, Mia. Everything's taken care of. Quinn's arranging transportation. Carolyn's contacted an event planner to handle the rest."

"You still need a hostess."

"I have a hostess." He put an arm around Laura's waist and drew her smoothly to his side. "And I can't wait for everyone to meet her."

Mia's gaze flicked over Laura, taking in her worn jeans and scarred jacket, her hair escaping its unfashionable braid. "Forgive me, but are you really used to managing an event of this kind?"

Laura opened her mouth to say that after corralling the drunks in the parking lot during the annual football rivalry between Eden High School and neighboring Fox Hole, she was pretty sure she could handle a room full of Scotch-sipping corporate types. But Simon cut her off.

"It's time for her to get used to it," he said, his arm tightening around her in warning. To his stepmother, they must look like a pair of regular lovebirds. Laura wasn't sure if she felt championed or annoyed. "But we appreciate the offer."

"I'd be happy to help," Mia said.

"Thanks," Simon said. "But all you have to do this time is show up and enjoy yourself."

Laura watched him smile at his stepmama, watched Mia's smile bloom in return. For a science geek, he was pretty smooth. Who'd have thought?

"Was there anything else?" Simon asked.

"I suppose not."

"Then we'll let you go. Nice of you to stop by."

Taking Mia by the elbow, he finessed her to the door and turned her over to Carolyn. The lock clicked shut behind her.

Laura blew out a breath. "Damn, you're good."

She would have to watch that.

"I've had a lot of practice," Simon said.

"Oh, really?"

"Yeah, I…" He met her gaze, an arrested expression in his eyes. "I remember that. I remember her."

She stomped on a nasty and completely inappropriate squiggle of jealousy. "What do you remember?"

"She had light hair," he said slowly. "And she was laughing. Except…" He shook his head. "Never mind. That wasn't Mia. That one had a baby, and Mia didn't want children."

"Your stepmother didn't want children," Laura repeated.

"Not someone else's," Simon said reasonably. "None of them did."

Anger curled in Laura's stomach. "Then why did they marry a man with a child?"

Simon looked surprised. "Our lives didn't really intersect, my father's and mine. He traveled a great deal. And I…" Memories deepened his eyes. "It doesn't matter now."

"It might," Laura argued. "If you remember something that could impact the investigation."

He arched his eyebrows. "You think I was hit on the head by the ghosts of my past?"

"Don't be clever. Talk. How old were you when your mother died?"

"I don't remember."

"So you were probably young."

"Or I don't remember."

Laura tried to find another opening. "You had four stepmothers. Do you remember them?"

"I… Dylan's mother," he said. "She was the blonde with the baby."

Excitement skittered along Laura's nerves. She did her best to ignore it. The quickest way to screw up an interview was to lose impartiality. "Was she the first?"

Simon nodded, his expression curiously smooth and young. "Kathy had Dylan. Amber had little dogs. Poodles, I think. Sharyn had Julie."

Laura hid her distaste for these women who had babies and puppies and no time for a bright, solitary little boy. Feeling sorry for the child Simon had been made no difference to him then and wouldn't help him now. At least he remembered something. "Tell me about Julie."

"Julie is my... My God," he breathed.

"Julie is your what?"

Simon lifted his head, realization dawning in his eyes. "Julie is my sister. Half sister. My younger half sister."

Bingo. "The girl in the photograph."

"Maybe."

"You're not sure?"

"I remember a baby. I didn't have anything to do with her. I wasn't supposed to have anything to do with her. But..."

Laura bit her tongue.

"She was crying," Simon said slowly. "I was home from school—it must have been spring break—and I heard her screaming for the longest time. I don't know why the nanny didn't come. So I went in to make sure she wasn't going to choke to death or something, and when she saw me..."

"When she saw you," Laura prompted.

"She was standing in her crib. And she put up her arms. You know, so I would pick her up."

She could almost picture them, the dark-haired, awkward boy, the red-faced, crying toddler. The image wrenched her heart. "And did you?"

"Yeah." He hunched his shoulders, a boy's gesture. "I

guess she followed me around after that. For a couple of weeks. Until I went back to school."

It was a poignant picture. "You remember that."

"I remember," Simon said quietly.

"You don't sound very excited about it."

"It's not a particular useful memory."

"Or a happy one," she guessed.

His face matured. Sharpened. "So when is a fifteen-year-old happy about anything?"

Laura frowned. "You were fifteen when you went away to school?"

"Nine, I think. It was easier for everyone if I was at school."

She'd heard worse. Seen worse. Abandoned babies, neglected or abused children and runaway teens were all part of her job. But Simon's matter-of-fact tone pressed against her breastbone like a knife.

"What about vacations? Holidays?"

"I told you, my father traveled."

She understood his defensive dismissal. Understood it and saw through the door. She'd made excuses for her father, too. "So you were alone a lot, huh?"

"I enjoy being alone," he said, looking down his long, straight nose at her. "I wanted them to leave me alone."

Maybe, Laura thought. But she'd done enough juvie work to know it was the kids who said they didn't want anyone who needed someone the most.

"What else do you remember?"

His mouth tightened. "Nothing."

"Anything about the night you were attacked?"

"No."

That figured. Everything he said was consistent with what Laura had read about retrograde amnesia. Older memories were usually the first to return, and the victims of trauma sometimes never remembered the time of their accidents.

But she had to keep an open mind. Just because she felt sorry for him, for the little boy he had been, was no reason to take everything he said at face value. Anything a detective learned in an interview had to be evaluated in the light of the available facts.

And at the moment Laura had damn few facts and way too many feelings. She wanted to trust Simon, and that alone made her suspect him and her own instincts.

He could be telling the truth.

Or he could have read the same sources she had.

She owed it to herself and to the investigation to stay impartial. But she was more moved than she wanted to admit by the images of his childhood.

"So, when can you get out of here?" she asked.

Simon looked surprised. She didn't blame him. She'd surprised herself. "Why?"

"You said you'd come with me when I went back to talk to my father's neighbors. What time can you leave?"

He smiled suddenly, and her heart did a slow roll in her chest and then soared. Jeez.

"I'm my own boss," he said. "I can leave right now."

Laura moistened her lips. This was an investigation. Not a date. There was no reason to feel that little flutter in her stomach. "Don't you have stuff to take care of first?"

"Since I don't know what I'm doing, it probably won't hurt to put off doing it for another day. Give me a minute with Carolyn, and we can go."

Carolyn required more than a minute.

Laura sauntered to the window and stood looking out as Simon's assistant presented him with letters to sign, appointments to approve, decisions to make. She listened, impressed, as he questioned, juggled and deflected, wondering if she'd made another big mistake. Simon Ford didn't need her pity. He didn't seem to need much of anything.

"Move the meeting with Macon to next week," he instructed Carolyn. "And tell Dylan I'd like another copy of that marketing report."

At last he pocketed his PDA and opened the office door. "Sorry to keep you waiting."

Laura strolled out. "No problem. It was interesting."

Simon caught up with her in two long strides and slipped an arm around her waist. She stiffened.

"Interesting, how?" he asked.

He was acting, Laura reminded herself. Playing a role for Carolyn and the earnest young man behind the front desk. Her foolish fault if it felt like more. She forced herself not to pull away.

"You're quite an operator," she said.

Simon's mouth twitched. "Is that a compliment on my job performance?"

His hand was warm on her back as he steered her to the elevator. Laura cleared her throat. "It's a comment on your performance, yes."

The elevator car seemed smaller going down, cramped, filled with the scent of Simon's aftershave and the warmth of his body. As soon as they reached the lobby, Laura bolted from under his arm, her boots echoing on the marble floor.

He tugged her back gently. "Are those the guards who harassed you?"

She glanced at Tweedledee and Tweedledum, ranked like bowling pins at their post. "What does it matter? Let's go."

Simon looped his arm across her shoulders. "This will only take a minute," he promised, and dragged her to the guard station.

Damn it.

Laura had no intention of providing the lobby staff with a repeat performance of the afternoon floor show. But unless she dropped him, she had no choice but to go along.

One guard nudged the other as they approached, and both straightened hastily.

"Is there a problem, Mr. Ford?"

"That's what I'm trying to figure out, Officer…" Simon's gaze flicked to the guard's badge. "Williams. And Cooper. I believe you've already met Ms. Baker."

"Yes, sir," Tweedledee—Williams—said.

The younger guard, Dwayne Cooper, shifted his weight, his gaze going to Laura. "What does she say?"

Laura stared him down. "I told him you apprehended me as I attempted to bring a concealed weapon onto the premises."

"Yeah." The guard nodded. "Uh, yes, sir."

"Ms. Baker is a friend of mine." Simon lowered his voice. "A close, personal friend of mine. Her safety and comfort are very important to me. I'm sure you understand."

Laura gritted her teeth.

Dwayne Cooper smirked. "Yes, sir."

Simon stepped closer. Into his space. Into his face.

"You touch her again," he said quietly, "you say anything to give her a hard time, you fail to cooperate or even look at her funny, and the next time that alarm goes off it will be because I've thrown you through the door. Is that clear?"

The guard stared straight ahead, his face sullen and red. "Yes, sir."

"Good." Simon stepped back. "Then there's no problem."

Laura was livid as she stalked through the tall steel-and-glass doors. "What do you think you were doing back there?" she hissed as they hit the sidewalk.

"Looking after you."

She ignored the flush of pleasure his words gave her. She couldn't remember the last time somebody had tried to look after her. Had dared to stand up for her. "I can look after myself."

"Indisputably."

She scowled. "Don't use big words in that snotty tone of voice. You acted like I'm some little woman in need of your protection. That's not who I am."

"It's who you're supposed to be. I'm giving credibility to your cover as my girlfriend."

He was right. That didn't make his protective act any easier to take. As Eden's only female officer, she wouldn't last two weeks on the job if she couldn't handle herself. She couldn't afford to let Simon fight her battles. It was bad for her image. And dangerous to her heart.

She turned on him. "You can't tell me you didn't enjoy that macho crap."

Simon smiled. "No, I can't tell you that. Is this your car?"

She looked down at her ticket-me-red Grand Prix GT, her one vanity and indulgence. "Yeah. Where are you parked? You can follow me in your car."

"I could if I wanted to leave Quinn stranded at the office. He drove me into work this morning," he explained blandly.

Laura narrowed her eyes. Was he manipulating her? Surely Simon Ford had the means and money to arrange alternate transportation for his driver. But the last thing she wanted was to get involved in more explanations and delays. Besides, he didn't know where they were going.

She unlocked the doors. "Fine. Get in."

Simon reached for the door handle.

"I'll drive," she snapped.

He swung the door open and held it for her. "I wouldn't have it any other way."

Chapter 8

"You can't get in," the building super repeated, shifting his considerable bulk in the doorway. A Chicago Bears T-shirt strained over his gut. From the stains on the shirt and the beer in his hand, Laura guessed they'd interrupted his dinner. "I can't hand out keys to anybody who asks for them, you know."

The scent of greasy french fries mingled with the tinny roar of the Cubs game drifting from inside the apartment. Laura hadn't eaten all day, and her hunger added another edge to her discomfort. Her stomach rumbled. She wondered if Simon heard.

"I'm not anybody," she said tightly. "I'm Pete's daughter."

"He never mentioned you."

Funny, how that still had the power to hurt after all these years. "He didn't mention you, either. That doesn't mean you aren't who you say you are."

The super snorted. "You got ID?"

She pulled out her driver's license and offered it to him.

He squinted at it. "How come you don't have the same last name?"

She was uncomfortably conscious of Simon listening behind her. "I married," she said shortly. "Swirsky's my maiden name."

"Huh." The super peered again at the license. "You sure don't look like him."

"Thank God for that," Simon said.

The man cracked a laugh. "Good one. Can't let you in, though." He handed back her license. "Not unless you got a badge and a warrant."

The way he said it made Laura think he'd been through the drill before. Her stomach sank. Of course Palmer had been here. In his shoes, she would have done the same. Looking for the rubies. Or the security tapes.

"You've spoken to the police?" she asked.

The super's face shuttered. He started to close the door. But Laura's foot was already over the sill.

"I don't want any trouble," he said.

"Good," said Laura. The edge of the door pressed against her boot. "Did the police already search the apartment?"

"He had a warrant," the super said.

Simon flattened his hand against the door, relieving the pressure on her foot. "I have something for you, too."

The man fell back. "I don't want any trouble," he repeated.

"No trouble," Simon assured him. He reached past Laura with his other hand, and she caught the flash of folded bills. What did he think he was doing?

Greed sparked in the super's face. He took the money; counted it. "What do you want?" he asked Simon.

"An hour inside," Simon said.

The man rubbed the bills between his fingers. There were at least three of them, and the outside one was a twenty. "Half an hour," he said. "And I keep the keys."

Simon looked at Laura. She nodded, her blood beating thick in her ears. She resented feeling like an imposter: not quite a daughter, not really a girlfriend, not officially a cop. She hated giving up control. But she was grateful to Simon for getting them inside, and relieved she wouldn't have to compromise her principles by flashing her shield.

Who was she kidding?

She was compromising her principles just by being here.

"Half an hour," Simon agreed. "And you leave us alone inside."

The man smirked. "Just don't get the sheets dirty."

He pulled a ring of keys from his pocket.

"You paid him too much," Laura said as soon as the door closed behind the super.

Simon waited until the man's footsteps faded away in the hall outside. Laura stood in the middle of her father's living room, her shoulders hunched and her chin at a dangerous angle.

He raised his eyebrows. "You want to go after him? Ask for our money back?"

She didn't smile. "It's not our money. It was your money. And you shouldn't have given it to him."

"I can afford it."

"That's not the point."

He knew that, just as he'd known any bending of the rules would bother her. Which was why he hadn't told her about it beforehand.

"You're not on the clock now, Detective. And I'm not on the payroll. Let's not make too big a deal out of a simple business transaction."

She flushed. "I'm not objecting to your methods. I've paid for information before. And I'm telling you he would have let us in for fifty."

Simon couldn't keep the amusement from his voice. "You wanted me to haggle with him?"

"No, I wanted…" She scowled. "Forget it."

"You wanted everything to be open and aboveboard and for him to let us into the apartment as a gesture of trust and good citizenship," Simon guessed.

"Are you making fun of me?"

"Actually I admire you for holding yourself to a code of conduct. Unfortunately the rest of the world doesn't play by your rules."

"That's what keeps the police in business. What rules do you play by?"

"I don't know." Fear gnawed at him, fear of all he'd forgotten and of what he might find out. He forced himself to speak lightly. "I don't even remember the name of the game."

Laura turned her head and stared at him, those clear brown eyes seeking. "You're doing fine."

"Right." His mouth twisted. "Any time you need to bribe someone, you let me know."

She cocked her head. "'Don't make such a big deal out of a simple business transaction.'"

She took two steps toward him, balancing on the balls of her feet, graceful as a dancer or a fighter. He eyed her warily.

"Thanks for the help," she said, and stood on tiptoe, and brushed her lips against his cheek.

He went hard as a rock and dumb as a stone. *Idiot. Moron.* You'd think a woman had never touched him before with simple affection.

Maybe none had.

He struggled to find breath, voice, perspective. "I only bought you half an hour," he said, relieved he didn't croak.

She nodded. Stepped back. "Then I'd better make the most of it."

He stayed rooted to the rug, frozen with lust and disappointment, as she circled the room, her hands in her pockets. He tried to see it through her eyes, the squat, brown furniture, the bare, white walls. A large TV occupied one corner of the room, but there were no plants, no pets, no personal objects beyond the stack of magazines in one corner and the pile of circulars on the desk.

It was depressingly like his house. Without the view.

He shook the thought away. "What are you looking for?"

"Swirsky's missing, right? Or on vacation." Simon noticed she didn't say "my father." "Except the old man never took a vacation in his life that didn't involve sitting in front of a game with a beer in his hand. I'm looking for signs that will tell me how long he's been gone, if he planned to be gone, if he expected to come back."

She stopped by the desk, perusing the monthly planner that lay open at the top, rifling through the correspondence. Not paying attention to Simon at all.

"Don't you have to worry about fingerprints?" Simon asked.

"This isn't a crime scene. Anyway, Dan's already been here. The bonus is since I'm unofficial, I'm not bound by plain view doctrine. I don't have to testify to what I see or how I found it. Though if I find anything suspicious, you can bet the chief will get an 'anonymous' tip."

Her hands continued their quick, neat shuffle. "Nothing here. No out of town receipts, no mysterious appointments. His address book is missing, but Dan probably took that. Let's check the bedroom."

Simon trailed her down the hall and stood in the doorway

while she opened drawers and closets. She'd slipped into her detective role as comfortably as her old leather jacket. Both looked good on her. Simon, watching, chafed in his suit and tie.

"What will you do if you find the rubies?"

"I won't." She got down on her hands and knees to look under the bed.

It didn't take a scientist to observe she had an excellent butt, lean lines and smooth curves packed in tight denim. He tugged at his collar.

"Ah...how can you be so sure?"

Her butt wiggled backward. *Really* excellent.

"Number one, because the old man didn't take them. Number two, if they were here, Dan would have found them and notified you your property had been recovered." She sat back on her heels.

With an effort, Simon refocused on her face. What were they talking about? Had she caught him staring?

"Plenty of dirty laundry and two empty suitcases," she reported. "I don't think Pete would leave town without clean underwear, so he didn't pack for a trip."

Simon wasn't particularly interested in her father's underwear. He was still trying to decide if the unbroken sweep of denim at her hip indicated she was wearing a thong.

She opened the drawer of the nightstand. "He used to keep a gun by the bed."

"Did you find it?" Simon asked, hoping his voice betrayed only a mild academic interest. She wasn't going to shoot him for staring, for God's sake.

"No. Just some ammo in the closet. He must have the gun on him."

Simon pulled his thoughts together. "Unless your Detective Dan confiscated that, too."

"Not likely."

"But isn't it evidence?"

Laura stood, wiping her hands on her jeans. "Of what? Gun ownership? You weren't shot. You were hit on the head."

"Lucky for me," Simon murmured.

But she had already disappeared into the bathroom.

Simon understood her absorption in her work. Recognized it. Respected it. Didn't he feel the same thing when he was in the lab?

And yet a part of him—ego, maybe, or libido—was ticked off she could dismiss him so completely from her mind.

He wanted her back. He wanted her with him. Not just physically—his mind veered briefly to thong panties—but mentally and emotionally as well. He wanted her leaning into him, looking up at him with softness in her eyes. *Thanks for the help.*

He should help her more. If only he could remember...

Leaving his post by the door, he wandered across the room to the tall, square dresser. A smear of ink and a spill of coins decorated the oak veneer top. Beside the plain black phone was a cheap metal frame with a single photo: two children on a beach. Simon picked it up.

A girl and a boy stared at the camera, surprised in their play. The girl was thin-faced, sober, with clear brown eyes and hair the color of tarnished brass. *Laura.* From the shovel in her hand, Simon guessed she'd been digging some kind of fort in the sand, erecting a wall against the rippling water. The boy, perhaps four or five years younger, crouched inside the hole.

Laura's voice came back to him. *Listen, I've got a kid brother, too. And God help us both if I tried to take responsibility for him.*

He should have returned Dylan's call earlier today, Simon thought, and set the frame down.

The light on the answering machine was on. Not blinking. No new messages, then. But something was stored on the machine.

Simon glanced toward the open bathroom door. Laura hadn't told him not to touch anything. He pressed the play button.

"It's Paul." A young man's voice, aggressively uncertain. "Are you there?" The tape hissed for a moment. "Okay, call me."

Laura appeared, backlit by the bathroom light. "Who was that?"

"Who's Paul?" Simon asked.

"My brother. How…" Her gaze fell to the answering machine. "Did he call?"

"Friday morning at ten o'clock," Simon said promptly, giving the time on the tape. "He left a message."

Frowning, Laura re-played the tape.

"All right, clue me in," Simon said. "Why is it a problem if your brother calls your father?"

"It's not."

"Fine." Something was wrong. She was keeping something from him. The knowledge made his gut churn. He trusted her. He wanted to trust her. "Would he know where your father is?" he asked evenly.

"He might."

"Were they close?"

"Yes. No. Dad got Paul his job."

"That sounds close to me."

"Not really. It was Dad's way of keeping Paul out of trouble. Of keeping tabs on him. Of keeping control."

Her tone was bitter.

Simon proceeded cautiously. "Did your brother need to be kept under control?"

"Dad certainly thought so. Well, to be fair, Paul rebelled some after our mother died."

"What about you? Did you rebel, too?"

"No." She shook her head. "No, I was the good girl who followed all the rules."

Simon could relate to that. Not that he remembered anyone who had cared enough about him to lay down rules beyond "Put down the toilet seat" and "Don't bother me now." But he used to make up his own rules, imagining that if only he followed them, if he was good enough, if he was *perfect*, someone would notice.

They never did.

Laura shrugged. "Of course, then I broke the really big rule and got pregnant, and poor Paul was really stuck."

"That must have been hard on you," Simon said inadequately.

"Harder on him." Her face took on the earnest expression of the girl on the beach, throwing up a bulwark between her brother and the water. "There was no one left at home to run interference. No one to talk to. I couldn't even call if Dad was in the house. He didn't want me to talk to Paul. And then as Paul got older, he didn't want to talk to me."

Had he worried she was keeping things from him? Everything she felt was on her face, the responsibility, the loyalty, the guilt. She was being so honest it hurt.

"Teenage boys can't talk to anyone," Simon said.

Even with the bump on his head, he remembered that much.

"I still should have been there for him."

"And your father should have been there for both of you. Give yourself a break."

She stiffened. "You don't know anything about it."

Simon was no expert on emotions. He didn't have a degree in psychology. But he could look at the facts and draw conclusions as well as anyone.

"You're right. I don't. I sure as hell never did much for my brother. And at seventeen, I couldn't have cared less."

"You gave him a job."

"I was in a position to give Dylan a job. The same way your father got your brother a job. You weren't in a position to do anything. You didn't have the money. You didn't have the authority. And you didn't have the time."

Her eyes widened. "The time."

"Yes. Between work and school, you must have—"

"No, I mean…the *time*." She pushed past him. "I only have thirty minutes, and I haven't searched the kitchen yet."

Simon was left alone in the empty bedroom. He looked at the girl in the picture frame.

"Why do I get the impression you would rather investigate my past than discuss yours?" he asked her.

But she had no answers for him.

Pete Swirsky's kitchen was clean, his dishwasher empty and his refrigerator nearly bare.

Simon glanced over Laura's shoulder at a half loaf of bread and some mustard, a jar of pickles and three cans of beer. "Looks like he planned on being gone for a while."

"Are you kidding? You should see the inside of my fridge." She swung the door shut, peered into the empty garbage can, scanned the counter by the phone. "Okay, I've seen enough. We can go."

Simon kept his eyes on her face. "You think he's coming back."

Her jaw firmed. "I'm keeping an open mind."

"Will you call your brother?"

"It's the next obvious step."

He was concerned. Not for the investigation, but for her. "But will you?"

She was saved from answering by a noise from the entrance. Keys rattled. The door scraped open.

Laura strode toward the hall. "I don't need you to tell me

how to do my job." She nodded curtly at the super. "We're done."

The fat man leered. "That was fast."

Laura leveled a look at him, direct and deadly as the muzzle of a gun.

The super shuffled back a step. "That is, uh…"

She reached inside her jacket, and he paled. Even Simon, who knew better, was mildly alarmed.

Her hand came out holding a plain white business card. She flicked it toward the super. "If anybody else comes by looking for my father, I want you to let me know."

"I'll see that you're compensated for your trouble," Simon added smoothly.

Laura's brows drew together in annoyance, but the man took the card.

Outside on the dirty street, she said, "You paid him enough already."

"Probably."

"You pay an informant too much, they make stuff up to collect the payment."

"And if I didn't pay, he might not call at all."

"Yeah." She sighed and unlocked the car doors. "I guess I should thank you again."

"You don't need to thank me." Simon waited until they were both inside the car before he added, "But you can kiss me again if you want."

Startled, Laura turned her head.

He returned her look blandly. His face was strong and impassive, only a hint of a smile in his eyes.

Against her will, she felt a fizz of amusement, a buzz of something else. Her heart thumped.

"I haven't had much luck necking in parked cars." Her voice was oddly breathless.

"Maybe your luck has changed," he suggested.

Possibility quivered through her. Simon stretched out in the seat beside her, tempting as a candy bar in the take-out line of the grocery store. He was smart, rich, reliable. Interested in her, if the glint in his eyes was more than a reflection of the light from the dash.

The buzz in her blood increased to a hum.

Could her luck really have changed?

She thought about it as she released the emergency brake, as she compared the temptation beside her with the recent direction of the rest of her life.

Consider the evidence. Review the facts. Her boss had just removed her from a high-profile case. Her old man, after staying conveniently out of her life for the past ten years, was back as the lead suspect in a half-million dollar theft. She needed to call her brother, who still hadn't forgiven her for abandoning him, and question him about their father's probable whereabouts. And after doing her damnedest for the past five years to prove herself as the equal of every man on the force, she was currently masquerading as the girlfriend of Eden's most famous citizen.

Nope, she decided regretfully. Fizzes and tingles aside, her luck hadn't changed at all. Unless it had gotten worse.

"I don't think so." She fastened her seat belt. "The last time I steamed the windows in a car, I wound up pregnant."

Simon didn't say anything.

She sneaked a glance at him at the next traffic light. He didn't look mad. Or shocked. Or disappointed, damn it. He looked…abstracted. Like he was thinking about something.

Genius boy, she thought scornfully, but it didn't have the sting she hoped for. It was hard to despise the wizard responsible for building Wonderland into the side of a hill. A guy who, like it or not, had stood up for her and stood by her. A man who had confessed the loneliness of his childhood and comforted her for the loss of hers.

Her chest squeezed. Oh, hell. She had to get rid of him before she did something she'd regret.

"Where can I drop you off?"

Simon's shadow stirred against the door. His knee brushed the console. "Are you driving back to Eden tonight?"

She came to a full stop at the red light before turning right. Some cops took advantage of the general reluctance to write a fellow officer a ticket, but not Laura. Laura played by the rules.

"Do I have a choice?" she asked.

"You do. I have a condo by Grant Park overlooking the lake. Three bedrooms," he added before she could say anything. "You're welcome to spend the night."

She was tempted, and by more than the man beside her. A free night in luxury digs wasn't something that came her way very often. She'd been up since five that morning, and she was tired. Which made it even more imperative she keep her guard up.

"No, thanks."

"Do you mind my asking why?"

I'm terrified of making another mistake.

"I have work in the morning," she said. "Besides, I didn't pack a toothbrush."

"Another time, then," he said equably.

She aimed a look at him.

"We are supposed to be involved," he pointed out. "It only makes sense that we would spend time together."

"Where other people can see us, yeah."

"You want to spend the night where people can see us? I'll check us into a hotel. I'm sure the desk could even provide a toothbrush."

Her pulse spurted. "Very funny. What's your address?"

"You don't need it. I'm coming to Eden with you."

To tell the truth, she would be glad of his company. Any company, she corrected herself. It was a long commute at the end of a very long day. But…

"What about Quinn?"

Simon shrugged. "He has the car. He can spend the night here."

Faint alarm bells sounded in her brain. "Oh, no. We still haven't caught whoever conked you on the head. You can't spend the night on the island by yourself."

"There's a solution for that."

"You want me to put you in protective custody at the jail for the night?" she asked.

He laughed softly. The sound shivered across her skin. "I was going to invite you to spend the night with me."

Hoo boy. But it was just a line. This was all a game to him. A pretense.

"Sleep across your threshold with my sword drawn?" With an effort, she kept her voice light. "No, thanks."

"How about in my bed with your gun under your pillow?"

Okay, that was still a line, but he wasn't pretending anymore. At least, she didn't think he was. Her heart thumped.

She shook her head. "Too dangerous."

Simon reached across the seats and skimmed his knuckles down her cheek. "I'm willing to take the risk."

Her insides melted. Her hands tightened on the steering wheel. "Well, I'm not. I am risk-averse. Contrary to what you might think about cops, we do not go around deliberately putting ourselves in danger. Well, maybe the adrenaline junkies do, the SWAT team guys and the bomb squad, but most of us keep our heads down and our feet dry."

"Is this a lecture on safe sex, Detective? Because I'm more than willing—"

"This is not about sex," Laura snapped. "That is, it is, but…" She stared out the windshield at the lights streaking by on Lake Shore Drive. "A good cop doesn't enter a scene without identifying the problem zones and deciding on an appropriate course of action."

"You made the problem zones very clear the last time I kissed you."

She blew out her breath. "Yeah. The thing is, I haven't decided what to do about you yet."

"Fine." His shadow shifted against the passenger side window.

"What are you doing?"

Simon held up his cell phone. "Calling Quinn to tell him to meet us at the marina in Eden. Will that satisfy your concerns for my safety?"

Laura wasn't used to having a man take her so completely at her word. Not her colleagues on the force, not her occasional dates. It made her feel good.

It kind of pissed her off.

"I don't see why you don't just have me drop you off here," she said rather sulkily.

"Because I would rather spend the hour and a half it takes to drive to Eden with you than with Quinn."

Oh. It was stupid, she decided, to feel flattered by that. "You want a chance to talk about the investigation? Or the party?"

"We should certainly discuss arrangements for Saturday." Simon's smile flashed in the darkness. "But what I actually want is the chance to change your mind."

Chapter 9

The car interior wrapped them in warmth and the comforting, familiar scents of takeout burgers and bad coffee. Outside, a dog barked. A radio played, bluesy and low, on one of the boats berthed at the dock. Moths committed suicide runs on the lights in the harbor, giving their lives in tiny bursts and flashes of light.

But inside the car, it was quiet and dark. Intimate.

Simon crumpled a napkin and tucked it into a bag. He was the neatest stakeout partner Laura had ever known. "You don't have to stay," he said. "Quinn will be here any minute."

Laura cradled her coffee cup in her hands, comfortable in her car. "Uh-uh. I'm not leaving till he gets here. I don't want to have any explaining to do if your body turns up in the lake tomorrow."

"I'm touched by your concern." His voice was a smile in the dark.

She rolled her head on the back of her seat to look at him. It was okay for Simon if his family and co-workers thought he was getting it on with one of the locals. They didn't live here. But she did. She'd parked in the shadows as much for concealment as for safety.

Still, what she could see of his silhouette was nice. Broad shoulders. Strong neck. His ears lay neatly against his head, and his hair was too long. She wanted to touch it.

Bad idea.

She cleared her throat. "You want to talk about the guest list for Saturday?"

"We could," Simon said agreeably. "If I'd brought a copy with me."

"Do you remember any names?" She caught herself. "Sorry. Bad question."

"That's all right. According to Carolyn, it's mostly senior management. Investors, lawyers, accountants. A few government contacts."

"Friends?"

Simon shrugged. "I told Quinn to include the people who are important to me."

No friends, Laura thought.

"You need to get a personal life," she said.

"I'm working on it."

She fought to ignore the flutter in her stomach. "Names," she said sternly. "Give me one name of somebody at that party you know personally."

"Kenny Gelb," Simon answered promptly. "I had lunch with him today."

"And he is…?"

"My chief financial officer."

"Doesn't count," she decided.

"Brian Walsh. Government grants and contracts," he added before she could ask.

She rolled her eyes. "Please."

"Dylan will be there," Simon offered, amusement rich in his voice.

"Also part of the company."

"And Mia."

His stepmother. Well, that was a personal relationship. Dysfunctional, maybe, but personal.

"That will make the evening special," Laura said dryly.

"I was counting on you to make the evening special."

She squinted at him. "Does that line work for you?"

"I don't remember," he deadpanned. "Is it working for you?"

Something was working for her, Laura acknowledged. Maybe it was the cocooning warmth of the car or the familiarity of the setting. Maybe it was the quiet dark or the fact that she'd finally been fed.

Maybe it was Simon. A frisson of alarm ran along her nerves. "We were talking about Saturday," she said.

"You were talking about Saturday." His shadow shifted against the window. "I was trying to change your mind."

"Then it's definitely not working," she lied.

"So I'll have to try something else." He leaned forward.

Her pulse picked up speed. She didn't have to sit here and take this. This was not part of their deal. This was a pretense. Or harassment.

He took her coffee cup away and placed it carefully on the dash. Her mind spun. Her nerves jangled. Now was a good time to remind him they were potentially working at cross purposes. Even though she'd promised to help him uncover his attacker, they couldn't just ignore that her father was a suspect. She needed to inform him that she called the shots in her relationships. She should tell him that if and when they got involved, it would be at a time and place of her choosing.

Threading his fingers through her hair, Simon pulled her closer. Her breath quickened.

Or she could Mace him.

His thumb brushed her lower lip, leaving her mouth moist and open. Aching.

He lowered his head. Her heart pounded.

His mouth fit hers as if they had been made for each other. His kiss was warm and firm. He tasted like coffee and, faintly, of ketchup, and he affected her system like a jolt of caffeine. She was dizzy. Breathless. Hungry for him, hungry for more. Hungry for everything.

Lifting his head, he looked at her, his eyes close and unreadable in the gloom.

She made a needy sound and reached for him again.

He came readily, leaning across the space between their seats, his arms strong and solid, his mouth sure and flatteringly urgent. She twisted closer, letting herself take and be taken, running her hands over him, arms, shoulders, chest, the smooth skin at the back of his neck just under his collar.

He went on kissing her, hotly, deeply, as he eased his hand under her jacket, shaping and stroking. She grabbed his hand and pressed it against her breast. Her nipple hardened under his palm. He rubbed her through her clothing and then she felt the brush of his knuckles, the play of his long, clever fingers as he slipped her buttons, one by one…

Light speared through the window, blinding her.

She jerked back as if she'd been shot.

"Baker? Is that you?"

Officer Paul Larsen's pale, good-natured face floated in the passenger side window. "I thought I recognized your car. What are you… Oh, hey."

Oh, hell, Laura thought, and grabbed for the edges of her shirt.

Simon moved to block the light, shielding her with his body. Too late.

Her bra was no-nonsense peach cotton, unnoticeable under her white shirt. Unnoticeable? She groaned. It was invisible in the dark. It must look like she wasn't wearing anything under her shirt at all.

Larsen grinned. "I didn't know you were on a stakeout tonight."

"You're a riot, Larsen." She sank into her seat, fumbling with her buttons in the dark. *Mistake, mistake, oh, God...*

"Who's with you?" The bright beam swung toward Simon.

"Put out the damn light," Laura snapped.

The flashlight bobbled and slid away. "Sorry," Larsen said, not sounding sorry at all.

Well, of course he wasn't. This was all a big joke to him. She'd been so careful to play by the rules, to hold herself aloof, never to do anything that would encourage the guys at the station to see her as a female instead of a fellow officer. And now she'd been caught breaking the ordinance against public displays of affection in a parked car on a public dock. Larsen probably couldn't wait for the end of his watch to get back and spread it around.

"I thought maybe you needed some help or something," he continued.

She struggled with the buttons. "No. Thanks, but—"

"Yeah, I can see you've got the situation in hand." Larsen chuckled.

Laura gritted her teeth.

He rested one arm on the roof of the car and leaned down, obviously prepared to stay and chat all night. "So, who's your date?"

Simon shifted to block Larsen's view of the interior of the car. "Simon Ford. Who are you?"

"Larsen. Paul Larsen. Wow. Are you really Simon Ford?"

"Yes." He pushed on the door handle. "Perhaps we could—"

Laura gripped his arm to yank him back. "Offer him money and you're a dead man," she growled in his ear.

He didn't even glance at her. "I appreciate your concern," he said smoothly to Larsen. "But everything is fine. We were just waiting for my driver."

"The guy over there?"

"What?"

Larsen jerked his thumb over his shoulder. "Big car under the lights. Is that your guy?"

Laura's face, her gut, her whole body burned. How long had Quinn been waiting? What had he seen? What must he think?

"That's him," Simon confirmed. "Very observant of you."

The cop grinned. "Guess I wasn't as, uh, distracted as you folks."

Guess not.

"It was nice to meet you," Simon said politely, dismissing him.

Larsen straightened. "Uh, yeah. You, too. Have a nice evening."

"Thanks," Simon said.

He waited until the officer strolled back to his patrol car before he turned to look at Laura. She'd managed to fasten all her buttons. He stifled a moment's regret.

"Are you okay?"

"I'm fine." Her face was pale. Her voice was tight. "Get out of the car."

"I can't," he told her ruefully.

"Yes, you can. Your ride's waiting."

He lifted an eyebrow. "Yes, he is. And unless you want him

to know exactly how kissing you affected me, I'm going to stay in the car another minute."

"Oh, God." She slumped in her seat. "I'm never going to live this down."

Okay, she was a little upset. He was going to have to deal with that if he wanted to get his hands on her again.

Which he did. Very soon.

"Don't worry about it," he said. "It's not that big a deal."

"Easy for you to say," she said bitterly. "Nobody thinks you're a slut."

More than a little upset. He had to proceed with caution.

"Do you want me to beat them up for you?"

She didn't laugh. "No. I can handle it."

Simon smiled at her. "Precisely my point."

She snorted.

Encouraged, he said, "This could actually work to our advantage."

"You think?"

"Yes. We wanted people to believe that we're involved. Now they do."

She stiffened. "Is that why you kissed me?"

Danger, danger, Will Robinson.

"I kissed you because I wanted to," Simon said carefully. He wanted to do a lot more than that, but this didn't seem to be the time to mention it. "I don't see that as a problem."

Laura tossed her head. "Then you're not looking at it very closely." But she sounded more sulky than mad.

He touched her, just her hand, his fingers tracing the delicate veins on the back. He figured more than that and she'd get uptight again. Or jab him in the ribs with her elbow.

"Don't worry," he said. "Everything's going to be all right."

* * *

But it wasn't all right, Laura thought the next morning as she slid into briefing ten minutes before her shift began at seven o'clock.

Veteran officer Charlie White was already there, sprawled comfortably at his tiny desk as he checked voice mail from his cell phone. Tim Clark, new to the shift and anxious to fit in, had his notebook and clipboard out, his coffee cooling before him. And loudmouth Larry O'Donal, who normally blew in as roll call started, was standing over both of them, laughing and punching the air with a breakfast biscuit.

At Laura's entrance, Charlie gave a slight, a very slight, jerk of the head. Tim looked down at his notebook, blushing. And O'Donal smiled around his biscuit like he was still hungry and she was breakfast.

Her stomach clenched. They knew.

Already.

Damn it.

She nodded to Clark and O'Donal, tested eye contact with Charlie. He smiled, his gaze sliding away. The knot in her stomach tightened. Oh, yeah, they knew.

"Little late this morning, aren't you, Baker?" asked O'Donal.

She sauntered to the coffeepot and poured herself a cup with hands that were barely shaking. "Not really. I thought you were early. Don't you usually scuttle in just in time to hear Denko read the hot sheets?"

O'Donal's grin broadened. "Speaking of hot sheets…"

Clark covered his laugh with his hand.

The lump in Laura's gut glowed like coal. The coffee was bitter in her mouth. The officers in the briefing room razzed each other all the time. They swapped jokes and war stories, shared training sessions and birthday parties, rehashed TV episodes and gossip. Getting grilled about last night's date made her one of the guys.

Except she wasn't one of the guys, and they all knew it.

The chief strode in from dispatch, the binders with the hot sheets under his arm. Laura took a seat, and the room settled.

Jarek Denko went through the lists for the day, pausing occasionally to instruct or explain: a suspicious person in the Glen Oaks development, a theft at the Bide-a-Wee cottages, garbage cans overturned and a shop window broken in the alley behind Highland Street. The officers nodded and jotted things down, what to watch for, where to go.

"Hey, Chief, what about extra patrols along the waterfront?" drawled O'Donal. "I hear there was some hot-and-heavy action going down on the marina last night."

Denko gave him a look that would have frozen lake water. "Focus on Highland Street today. I had three calls from merchants this morning."

"That's all the action O'Donal will see, anyway," Charlie White said, winking at Laura. "Barb's still making him sleep on the couch because he forgot their anniversary."

The rookie, Clark, sniggered. The tightness eased in Laura's gut. Okay, she was embarrassed, but she wasn't disgraced. As long as Charlie and the chief were willing to stick up for her...

Denko wrapped up and dismissed them. Laura shut her notebook and shuffled her things together.

"Laura?" The chief spoke quietly behind her. "Can I see you for a moment, please?"

Acid crawled up her throat. She cleared it. "Sure. Let me just get my equipment."

He nodded. "In my office. Five minutes." He left the suddenly silent room.

She carried her still full coffee cup to the trash and dumped it.

"Lau-ra's in trou-ble," O'Donal sang out.

"Get stuffed, O'Donal," she snapped, and stalked after the chief.

His office door was open. Denko sat behind his ugly desk, reading through the latest crime and missing persons reports to come in through dispatch.

"Laura." He welcomed her with a smile. "Close the door, will you?"

She took a deep breath and complied. "You wanted to talk to me, sir?"

"Yes. Before we get started, though…" He leaned back in his chair. "I wondered if there was anything you wanted to tell me."

There was nothing she wanted less.

She kept her hands still and her eyes steady. Denko was too good a detective to miss the small, betraying signs of guilt. "No, sir."

"Because if something was going on that I should know about," the chief continued, "I'd appreciate hearing it from you."

He was giving her the chance to explain herself. And she didn't have a clue what to say.

Denko sighed. "I'm not telling you what to do in your off hours. I know temptations can arise in the course of the job, and sometimes relationships develop."

Laura tried to remember how Denko had met his own wife, a reporter for the *Eden Town Gazette*. Teresa Denko— DeLucca, then—had covered that rape case a couple of years ago. And wasn't her brother a suspect or something?

So maybe the chief wasn't planning on throwing the book at Laura after all.

"Yes, sir," she said cautiously.

"But there is such a thing as being too personally involved

in your work." Denko frowned. "Which is why I removed you from the Ford case."

Her cheeks stung with humiliation. "Yes, sir."

"You are removed," he reminded her.

Laura lifted her chin. "You made that clear. Do you mind my asking how the investigation is coming along?"

"Actually, that's what I wanted to talk with you about. The computer printout you requested from E.C.I.P. came yesterday."

An ominous lump formed in her stomach. She waited.

"The record shows twenty-four master passcards created for Lumen Corp," Denko continued. "One for Ford, one for his brother, one for his butler, and twenty for the E.C.I.P. personnel assigned to Lumen Corp security."

"That's twenty-three," Laura said.

"An additional passcard was created for the guard covering your father's shifts," Denko said.

"The cards are individually coded," Laura said. "You should be able to look at the computer log to identify whose key was used to access the lab that night."

"We did."

The lump grew larger and more indigestible. She swallowed hard. "And?"

For once, Denko didn't quite meet her eyes. "The log shows two cards were used to gain entry that night. Simon Ford's and Peter Swirsky's."

The apprehension in her stomach grew so large it pressed her lungs, cut off her air. "Could someone else have used his key?"

"It's possible," Denko acknowledged gently. "I've directed Dan to continue to pursue all available leads. If the passcard turns up in someone else's possession, that would certainly help clear your father. And of course we're still waiting on the latest fingerprint report from DCI." The Illinois Department of Criminal Investigation, which did the lab work for their small department. "I'm sorry, Laura. But given the evidence of the log and his disappearance, Dan considers Peter Swirsky our lead suspect."

"I understand," Laura said evenly.

The chief's gaze sharpened. "Do you? I wanted you to know in case the information has any bearing on other…developments."

Her palms were sweating. "I haven't broken any regulations, sir."

Bent the rules, compromised her standards, flaunted his authority, sure. But she hadn't violated the law. Or interfered with the investigation.

Yet.

Exactly.

"I appreciate your dedication," Denko said dryly. "So your involvement with Simon Ford is…?"

"Personal," she said firmly.

A corner of Denko's mouth lifted in a near smile. "Are you reassuring me that you are not shadowing this investigation, or are you telling me politely to butt out of your private life?"

He was a good boss, Laura thought, her charade burning like an ulcer in her gut. He was giving her the chance to come clean. She owed him her best work and her loyalty.

But she felt a responsibility to her father, too. She'd given her promise to Simon. And she still hadn't figured out what she owed herself.

"He's throwing a party Saturday night," she blurted out. "He asked me to be his hostess."

"A party." Denko sat back, regarding her. "Do you know if he's made extra security arrangements?"

"Well." Laura cleared her throat; attempted a smile. "There's me."

"Ah."

He let the silence stretch a moment longer. A bead of sweat trailed down Laura's spine.

"That should keep you out of trouble," Denko said finally. "Have a nice time."

"Thank you, sir," she said, and escaped.

Chapter 10

She must have been out of her mind.

Standing like a princess on the balcony of Simon's personal castle, Laura touched her elbow to her waist, seeking the reassuring pressure of her gun. Except she wasn't wearing her gun. She was wearing a strapless sheath of lavender silk that had cost her three hours of searching and two weeks' pay, a bra that resembled a medieval torture device and sandals she couldn't run in. She'd even done girlie stuff to her face and hair. She felt self-conscious, half naked and utterly ridiculous. She'd spent her last date knocking down pins at the Thunder Bowl and beers at the Blue Moon. She couldn't remember the time or the man before that.

She took a deep breath of cool night air, making the top of her dress swell alarmingly, and exhaled on a sigh.

Below her, the boat ferrying guests from the marina bumped gently against the dock. A full bar was set up at the bottom of the walk beside golf carts waiting to transport Simon's guests to the house. A guitarist played under trees strung with fairy lights. The bright notes drifted up the hill, blending with the jazz trio playing her grandmother's music inside. The whole effect was elegant, extravagant…and intimidating as hell.

Lights bobbed and swayed on the water. She heard the whir of golf carts, the laughter of guests as they started up the hill, and something close to envy stirred in her heart.

She didn't want what they had, she told herself. Not their money or position, not their careless confidence or connections. But standing here between the moon and the fairy lights, in her slipping dress and uncomfortable shoes, stripped of her shield and her gun, she yearned for…something. Longed for something that sparkled just beyond the reach of her imagination, as beautiful and unattainable as the moonlight on the water.

"I thought I saw you come out here," Simon said behind her.

She turned, and caught the full force of him like a punch in the stomach: the hard planes of his face, the spare lines of his body, the cool flash of his eyes. He took her breath away. She saw stars.

It was the setting, she told herself. It was the suit. He looked good really in a monkey suit, like some movie star, austere and handsome in black and white. He was carrying two flutes of champagne—not the plastic kind where the bottom came off, either—and looked perfectly at home.

He was home. She was the one who was out of her element. Over her head.

She couldn't call herself a detective tonight. She couldn't call herself Simon's girlfriend, either. She was floundering in both roles, as uncomfortable with her charade as her shoes.

It was harder for Simon, she reminded herself. At least she knew her lines. He had to play himself without any script at all.

He handed her the sparkly wine and then touched his glass to hers. Acting, she thought with a little pang. If he never regained his memory and lost his career as a Tech God, he could make a fortune in the movies.

"Laura, I'd like you to meet a friend of mine," he said, gesturing to someone standing beside him.

That was her cue. He needed to know his friend's name. And she hadn't even noticed the guy. It was time she got over herself and concentrated on her job.

Transferring her glass, she stuck out her right hand. "Laura Baker."

Simon's companion pumped her arm a few times, making her bodice jiggle. "Bill Anderson."

Laura kept her smile in place. This whole gig was her idea. Her chance to ask questions without arousing suspicion. Her opening to dig discreetly into the motives and alibis, the organization and personalities behind Simon's corporation. "How do you know Simon, Mr. Anderson?"

"Call me Bill," he invited. "I'm working with Simon here on his muscular tetanization device."

Laura blinked. "His what?"

"You can use radiation to create a charge identical to the electrical impulses the brain uses to contract muscle tissue," Simon said quietly. "At the right frequency, the current stimulates the muscle fibers to a single sustained contraction. Tetanization."

She looked at him blankly.

"Temporary paralysis," he said.

"Phasers on stun," Bill added helpfully. "Like on *Star Trek*."

He wasn't kidding. Was he kidding?

"I guess it beats pepper spray," Laura said.

Bill chuckled as if she'd made a joke. "Indeed it does."

"Laura is in law enforcement," Simon said. If she didn't know better, she would have sworn there was a note of pride in his voice.

"Really?" Bill eyed her speculatively. "You'll have to talk Simon into letting you test the prototype, then."

"Yeah, next time I have to wrestle a three-hundred-pound drunk into the back of a squad car, I'm absolutely going to give him a call," Laura said.

Bill laughed. They stood around making business noises for a while before the other man excused himself.

Laura waited until he disappeared through the crowd before she turned to Simon. "Was he making that stuff up? About the, you know, phaser thing?"

"It's in development. For the Pentagon's Joint Non-Lethal Weapons Program."

Had she felt intimidated before? It was nothing to the way she felt now. He really was the Wizard King, and she was just Cinderella in too-tight shoes and a bodice that kept slipping.

"Jeez," she muttered. "I guess that explains why you're not so interested in making jewelry."

"The two projects aren't as far removed as you might think," Simon said. "They just utilize different lasing mediums. The solid state lasers use rubies. The MTD uses ionized channels in the air."

"You know, I don't mind playing dumb," Laura said to her champagne glass. "But I hate feeling stupid."

Simon frowned. "You're not stupid."

"I dropped out of high school."

"After your father kicked you out, I don't imagine you had much choice."

"Not much." But she didn't make apologies for it, and she didn't make excuses.

"So you earned your G.E.D.," he guessed.

She had, spending her days on her feet behind a cash register at the Jewel grocery store, spending her evenings hunched over her books on the scarred kitchen table, spending every waking hour struggling to keep her dingy apartment spotless and her reluctant young husband happy.

She shrugged. "Big deal. I bet you graduated at the top of your class."

"As you say, big deal." He kept those cool, observant eyes on her face. "Where did you go to college?"

"I went to night school."

"But you got your degree."

She nodded.

"I didn't finish college," he said.

"You didn't finish MIT. That's a little different from Lakeside Community College."

He looked down his long, straight nose at her. "I never realized you were a snob."

Indignation made her snap. "I'm not. I'm just saying, we're different."

"You're right. We are. You've had to work a lot harder to get where you are."

She felt a warm glow in the pit of her stomach that had nothing to do with alcohol. She'd barely touched her champagne.

"I'm going to have a tough time resenting your superior intelligence if you start acting all nice," she said crossly. "Knock it off."

"I have a tough time not saying nice things when you so obviously deserve them."

She was flattered and trying hard not to show it. "Oh, please."

"It's true. You're dedicated. Determined. Sharp. Good with people." With a single finger, he traced a line along her bare shoulder. She shivered. "And I like your dress."

The warmth in his eyes embarrassed her. She tugged on her bodice. "I feel like I'm working vice."

He cocked an eyebrow. "Undercover?"

"Under covered is more like it."

He laughed, and the tightness in her stomach eased. "You look beautiful," he said.

She opened her mouth, prepared to make another wiseass comment. She met his gaze and the words died. His eyes darkened. Her blood drummed in her ears. The moment stretched between them like a thread woven of music and spun with stars.

This, her heart whispered. This was what she wanted.

"Necking on the balcony, big brother? That is so unlike you."

Simon's brows snapped together in annoyance. "Dylan."

He strolled through the French doors, his blond hair silver in the moonlight, looking like the answer to every maiden's prayer. Laura wished he'd jump off the balcony.

"What are you doing here?" Simon asked.

"I was invited. Hi, Laura. Nice dress."

She struggled to get her breath, her balance, her composure back. "So your brother was telling me."

Dylan looked interested. "Did I butt in on a romantic moment?"

"Yes," Simon said. "Go away."

This was not what she was here for, Laura told herself. She should be glad Dylan interrupted them before she made another mistake. "Not really."

He grinned. "Maybe you need pointers on your technique," he said to Simon. "Come have a drink with me, darling," he invited Laura. "There are some things I do better than Simon."

Laura stole a glance at Simon. His face was a polite mask. His shoulders were rigid. He wouldn't object if she disappeared with Dylan for half an hour to pump him for information.

And she couldn't do it. She simply could not ditch Simon for his charming younger brother.

"His technique is fine," she snapped. "Yours could use a little work."

"I like her," Dylan said. "Definitely not a Stepford. Can we keep her?"

Simon stopped looking frozen and merely looked grim. "Don't you have someplace else you have to be?"

"Nope," Dylan said cheerfully. "I'm avoiding Mia. She's here with that bastard Macon."

"Who's Macon?" Laura asked so Simon wouldn't have to.

But he surprised her by answering. "Vince Macon. Big shareholder."

"Which means of course that his opinions are very important to us," Dylan said.

Bad blood there, Laura thought. Which was good. Maybe she'd find out something tonight after all. "Which opinions in particular are we talking about?"

"Simon!" The woman's voice, rich and modulated, reached across the balcony.

Dylan winced and Simon stiffened. In that instant, they looked more like brothers than they ever had before. Shoulder to shoulder, they turned to face a common foe.

Mia.

Instinctively Laura moved to protect them. It was ridiculous. They were grown men. But they hadn't always been, and Laura's heart ached a little for the boys they'd once been.

Mia glided toward them, a vision in red, flaunting her still firm body and a fortune in glittering stones around her neck.

"I should have known I'd find you in a corner. He always did hide at parties," she said to the distinguished gray-haired man beside her. "So awkward."

"Hello, Mia," Simon said quietly. His gaze flicked to her escort.

Laura squared her shoulders. She figured she could take out Mia in about thirty seconds, no phaser required. But Simon needed a different kind of protection tonight.

"Laura Baker," she said, offering her hand to the gray-haired guy, ruddy and confident in his tux. "It was so nice of you to come."

"Vince Macon," he said heartily. "I've heard a lot about you."

Her eyes slid to Mia, watching them with poorly concealed dislike. I'll just bet, Laura thought.

"That's so sweet," she said. "I've heard about you, too."

"Easy, Stepford," Dylan murmured. "Don't overdo it."

"Dylan." Mia exposed all her teeth when she smiled, like a cat. She looked pointedly at the glass in his hand. "Still sponging off your brother, I see."

He raised his drink in salute. "At least I work for the money he gives me. Love your necklace. Who paid for it?"

"This?" Mia's hand fluttered to her throat. Her smile widened. "A gift from a friend."

Laura took a closer look at the necklace. Some cop's sense clicked in her brain, like the sound of a door being closed down the hall. "Are those rubies?"

Mia preened. "Aren't they beautiful?"

"Beautiful," Laura agreed. "Are they real?"

Mia gaped. "Excuse me?"

"I'm sorry," Laura said, pretending confusion. "I just

thought since Simon's company makes, you know, synthetic gemstones—"

"Only as a by-product," Vince said. "Simon's laser research is too important to divert resources to an unprofitable sideline. It's a waste of time and money."

"Actually," Simon said slowly, "it doesn't take much time. Even with the slow growth method, the entire process doesn't take more than a few weeks."

Dylan lowered his glass to stare at his brother. "But you said—"

"The formula can be duplicated," Simon said. "The technology already exists. We can explore our options without it costing us anything."

Wait a minute. The stones were gone. Stolen. What was he trying to do?

"Vulcan Gemstones is still interested," Dylan said. "I can reschedule—"

"Not yet," Simon said.

Vince shook his head. "I hope you know what you're doing."

Simon smiled faintly. "So do I."

Laura waited until they'd all disappeared toward the music and lights inside before she rounded on Simon. "What was that about?"

He raised his eyebrows. "You said you wanted to bring together a specially chosen group of people and observe them in a controlled environment."

She remembered. "Like lab rats."

"Exactly."

"So?"

"So." He smiled. "I just reset the trap for you."

Her heart thumped and then sank. She scowled. "Using yourself as bait."

"Using the rubies as bait."

"I don't like it. It puts you at risk."

Simon shrugged. "Until we know who's responsible for the breach in my company's security, I'm at risk anyway. That's why you wanted this party."

"That was before," Laura said tersely.

Simon looked at her, slim and straight and shining like a blade in the moonlight, and lost his train of thought.

"Before what?"

"Before I…" She hesitated. "Knew you."

His mouth dried. Was that "know" as in, "tell me about your lousy childhood and I'll tell you about mine"? Or "know" as in, "let's get up close and naked"? Because if it was—please, God—the second, then she could get to know him better. Much, much better. They could…

Simon reined in his imagination. He needed data before he jumped to conclusions.

He cleared his throat. "Why would that make a difference?"

"Because now it's personal."

"Personal is not a problem for me," he assured her.

She cocked her head. "No?"

"All right, yes," he admitted, annoyed. "Obviously I suck at relationships. I don't have close ties to any of these people. I have no friends. My brother and I barely get along. I loathe my stepmother. But I'm trying, with you. You could consider cutting me some slack."

Her mouth dropped open. Closed. Opened again. "I didn't mean…I wasn't talking about your interpersonal skills, for God's sake. I'm talking about your safety. I don't want you to get hurt."

She was worried about him. He was touched.

And he didn't want to lose her sweet concern. He didn't want to lose her. The fear that he might troubled him more than any physical threat. Without Laura, he was alone in the sterile chill of his lab, in the isolation of his cheerless, colorless house, in the darkness of his own mind.

But he couldn't tell her so. He was perilously close to whining already.

"Then you'll have to take care of me, won't you?" he said.

She narrowed her eyes at him. "I can't take care of you if I'm…"

Horizontal?

Naked?

"…distracted," she said.

She was right. And he didn't give a damn. He wanted to hold her, keep her, bind her to him by any means necessary.

Sex, for example. Sex would be good. In fact, since Laura wouldn't let him buy her amazing loyalty with money, sex was probably his best option.

Lucky for him.

He took a step closer, close enough to smell her soap and skin and perfume, the scent subtle and a little spicy. It swam in his head. Removing the champagne flute from her fingers, he set it on a nearby table. "Am I distracting you?"

She moistened her lips nervously. But she didn't back down. Or back away. "You know you are."

"Good." He threaded his fingers through her hair, his touch deliberately light. The strands shone like liquid mercury and slipped like water through his hands.

She looked up at him, her eyes huge and dark, her angular face soft in the moonlight. "I'm serious."

"So am I," he said, and covered her mouth with his.

Her lips were slick and soft. She parted them, touching her tongue to his, kissing him back without caution or pretense, as direct in her desire as in everything else. She tasted sweet, delicious, like sex and champagne, and the combination of her hot, lush mouth and her cool, slim body sent him over the edge. His mind blanked with lust. His body burned.

Cupping her head, he stepped into her, easing one foot between her high-heeled sandals, thrusting his leg between her thighs. She trembled against him as he slanted his mouth, taking the kiss deeper.

Her hand clamped on his wrist.

Reluctantly he raised his head. "What?" he asked, hoping it was something he could deal with fast and get on with the good stuff.

Laura's mouth set. Her breathing was rapid. "Nobody's watching now."

He didn't get it. "That's good, right?"

Her throat moved as she swallowed. "You don't have to pretend. Nobody's watching."

He wanted to laugh. Or groan. Instead he pressed against her, letting her feel him through his heavy slacks and her light dress. Her eyes widened.

"Does this feel like I'm pretending to you?"

She swallowed again. "Uh, no. Guess not."

"I want you," he told her, and watched her eyelids flutter. "Not to solve the case. Not to save my ass. I want you."

She drew a shuddering breath. "I need to solve this case. And you need someone to protect your ass."

"So move in with me. You can provide me with round-the-clock protection."

Her chin came up. "I won't be pressured into having sex with you."

"I'm not pressuring you." She looked at him in obvious disbelief. He laughed, amused and caught out. "All right, maybe I am."

"I gave into pressure once before," she said. "And let me tell you, it was the biggest mistake of my life."

"Only once?"

She didn't smile. "Once was enough."

Simon's throat tightened. She couldn't actually mean there hadn't been anyone since…

"Your husband?"

"'I want you so much' sounds good when you're seventeen and want somebody to want you," Laura said. "But it's not enough anymore."

Hell.

"What do you want? Promises?"

It was a little early for that. They'd known each other barely a week. Right now Laura was as necessary to him as breathing. But when he regained his full memory, when he was himself again, would she want him?

A sharper fear sliced him. Would he want her?

She shook her head. Her hair brushed her bare shoulders. "I've had promises."

And from the tone of her voice, it was obvious she didn't put her faith in them anymore.

"What, then?"

"This isn't about what I want from you. It's about what I expect of myself."

"Okay," Simon said cautiously.

"There have been other men."

That was a relief. He frowned. Wasn't it?

"Not many," she added, perhaps misunderstanding the reason for his frown. "I make my own choices and I accept the consequences. If I have sex with you, I'll take full responsibility."

He'd like to think he'd have something to do with the decision, too. But he said, "That sounds reasonable."

Analytical. Logical. Too bad he wasn't in the mood for logic.

If I have sex with you.

The lightbulb went off, electrifying his body. "Does that mean we're going to have sex?"

Her cheeks flushed. He wanted to test their temperature with the backs of his fingers.

"Gee, that's really romantic," she said. "How could I possibly say 'no' after that?"

He was amused. Moved. And more uncertain than he'd been since he'd woken up on the floor of his lab. "Do you want romance, Laura?"

"No. I don't know. I told you, I'm responsible for my own choices. I don't need a bunch of flowers and pretty words to make up my mind."

He should have been relieved. It was interesting to discover he felt insulted instead.

"So, no romance," he said. "What am I supposed to offer you, then? Chemistry?"

She looked him in the eye. "I think we've proven chemistry is a factor."

"Any other requirements? Respect, for example?"

"Is this the part where you tell me 'you'll respect me in the morning'? Because I can do without that."

"No, this is the part where I tell you I have feelings for you," he said with an edge to his voice. "It's not all about getting you into bed, although maybe you'd like to reduce it to that. I respect you. I respect what you do. I admire what you've accomplished by yourself and for yourself without making a big deal out of it. I'm grateful you don't need to have everything explained to you. Although in this case, Detective, you're being a little slow on the uptake."

It was possible, Laura discovered, to be moved almost to tears and really pissed off at the same time.

"Well, thank you," she said, her voice shaking. She hated that. "Thank you so much."

Simon reached for her. "Laura…"

She raised both hands. In surrender? Or to hold him off? Even she couldn't say. "I'm not finished."

His hand dropped. "I'm listening."

She drew a painful breath. "The thing is, I have feelings for you, too. Respect and…feelings, okay? And they make me vulnerable. I'm not sure I like that."

Simon looked stunned, as if she'd just hit him over the head with one of his own deck chairs. "Well." He gave a short laugh. "That's honest."

She hunched her shoulders, feeling more naked and awkward than ever. If she'd had pockets, she would have put her hands in them. "Too honest."

"No." He regarded her thoughtfully, his eyes dark and unreadable. "We've now established we have chemistry, respect and honesty between us. I can't think of anything better to base a relationship on, can you?"

What about love? a small, rebellious voice inside her cried.

But of course she didn't say anything. There was honest, and then there was just plain stupid.

Besides, she'd stopped believing in love about the time she gave up her faith in fairy tales.

She managed a smile. "As long as we understand each other."

"Do we?" Simon murmured. "I wonder."

Laura shivered and hugged her arms. "We should go in."

"In a minute," Simon said.

Rubbing his warm hands up and down her bare shoulders, he cupped her elbows and tugged her gently closer.

Her breathing hitched. "I don't want to spoil the mood, smart guy, but there are lots of people we still need to talk to."

"Just a minute," he said, and kissed her.

He kissed her slowly, thoroughly and with exquisite care. She'd never been kissed quite like this, with the full focus of a man's attention, as if kissing her was something important, significant, that had to be done just right. Her head spun. Her knees wobbled.

And her heart, her poor heart, melted.

Simon raised his head and smiled into her dazed eyes. "Now we can go in."

Chapter 11

He still hated parties.

Simon propped a shoulder against the fireplace. Maybe he had overdone the my-home-is-my-castle thing in his former life. But at the moment the fifty or so remaining guests felt like unwelcome invaders. He'd tolerated their presence for the chance to set his trap and jog his memory. But now he wanted them to go away so he could be alone.

No, he admitted. He wanted them gone so he could be with Laura.

He watched her move among his guests, listening, smiling, asking questions, and his chest tightened with possessive pride. All night long, she'd had his back like a modern-day shield maiden, protecting him from hidden enemies and social disaster. Even if he had his full memory back, he wouldn't be able to connect with people the way she did.

Despite his frustration—with himself, with the situation,

with his failure so far to talk her into bed—they'd made progress tonight.

He remembered the glow of her face in the moonlight, her slumberous dark eyes when he'd kissed her, and anticipation buzzed in his blood. Definite progress.

And then disaster struck.

A sleek young blonde excused herself from a cluster of departing guests and flung herself at him, crying, "Simon! I've been looking for you everywhere."

He barely had time to register details—silver eye shadow and a shiny belly button ring that glittered through the gauze panel of her black dress—before she was in his arms.

Grimacing, he looked over her head for Laura.

She saw, of course, and came smoothly to his rescue.

Standing a yard away, her arms crossed over the bodice of her narrow purple dress, she put her head to one side and drawled, "If she's another stepmother, your father should be in jail."

The little blonde raised her head, laughter lighting her blue eyes. Some memory stirred in Simon, not in his mind, but in his heart.

"Oh, that's a good one," the blonde said approvingly. "You must be Laura."

"That's me," Laura said, and stuck out her hand.

The blonde ignored it, throwing her arms around Laura instead. "This is so cool. I couldn't believe it when Quinn called. Simon never invited me to meet any of his… Well." She laughed. "It's a pleasure to meet you."

Laura cleared her throat. "Julie?"

Julie?

Shocked, Simon studied the young woman embracing Laura. He'd expected his half sister to be a schoolgirl. This sparkly, confident blonde was twenty at least. But the shape of her eyes under her plucked and arched brows, the dimple flashing in her cheek, tugged at him. Did he recognize her from the high school photograph upstairs? Or was a deeper familiarity speaking?

"Julie," he said, testing her name in his mouth.

"Yeah?" She turned to face him. "Oh, don't scold. You should have figured I'd come."

"Come from where?" Laura asked.

"Didn't Simon tell you?" For a second, hurt flickered across the blonde's pretty face. And then she giggled. "Of course, you two probably have better things to do than talk about me. I'm at Moore College of Art and Design in Philadelphia. And I'm allowed three absences, Simon, which you know because I sent you the prospectus along with the tuition bill, and I haven't missed a class all semester, so you can stop looking disapproving."

He wasn't disapproving. He was stunned.

His sister liked him. His opinion mattered to her. One person in his life, it seemed, cared about him. There was one person he had cared for in return.

The relief was staggering.

"Did you do the painting over the fireplace?" Laura asked.

Julie rolled her eyes. "You mean, my early Kandinsky period? I don't know why Simon keeps that thing."

But Simon knew. Suddenly he remembered.

"I keep it because you gave it to me for my birthday, brat. And as astonishing as it may seem to your sophisticated tastes now, I like it."

She beamed. "Isn't he sweet?" she asked Laura.

Laura looked at him, warmth and something else in her eyes, something wary and shy that made his heart beat faster. "Tell me about it."

Her tone was dry, but Julie took her invitation at face

value. "Well, he rescued me from Sharyn. Sharyn's my mother. Did he tell you about her?"

"He mentioned her," Laura said.

Simon frowned. What the hell had he said? He didn't have many memories of Julie's mother. He'd already been away at school when his father had married again.

"Did he tell you he threatened to cut off her allowance if she kept me at that crappy boarding school? And then he came and moved me to the new school himself, and he let me spend part of the next two summers with him." Julie grinned. "Of course, he only agreed to that after I ran away about three times, but it was still sweet of him."

"I am not sweet," Simon said. "I was desperate."

His sister laughed.

Laura watched him, still with that wary, wondering look in her eyes. Simon wondered if she was remembering there had been no one to rescue her when she was Julie's age.

"You know he sucks at personal relationships," Laura said.

Simon winced.

Julie looked startled. "Who told you that?"

"He did."

"Well, he would," his younger sister said frankly. "Simon's not what you'd call touchy-feely. And he never did suffer fools gladly. But you can count on him to rescue you when things are really dire."

"Good to know," Laura said.

"Mr. Ford."

Quinn stood a yard away, stretching the seams of his navy blue suit, his round face creased with trouble and shining with sweat. A guard in a black E.C.I.P. uniform loomed behind him.

"It's all right, Quinn, I found him," Julie assured him cheerfully.

Quinn's gaze flickered to her and away. "Yeah, I can see that. Mr. Ford, we have a—"

"Problem?" Laura asked quietly.

"Situation," Quinn said. "Down at the dock."

A prickle of foreboding ran across Simon's shoulders. He'd meant to set a trap tonight. But it was too soon, much too soon, to catch anything. "Did someone fall in?"

Quinn rubbed his square hand over his face. "You could say so."

Julie's dimple deepened. "What do you mean, 'you could say so'? Was there a splash?"

"How long ago?" Laura asked.

Quinn looked at Simon. "If I could talk to you for a minute privately, sir."

"Julie, who did you come with tonight?" Simon asked.

"Dylan. But—"

"Why don't you go find him?"

She huffed. "That is so lame. Like sending me to my room."

But she blew him a kiss, said a warm goodbye to Laura and sashayed across the room.

"Go ahead," Simon said grimly.

Quinn rolled his eyes toward Laura. "What about—"

"If there's a situation, I'm better qualified to handle it than anybody here," Laura said crisply. "What happened?"

He admired the no-fuss way she stepped up and stepped into her role as a law enforcement officer.

"There's been an accident," Quinn said. "One of the boats taking guests back to the marina."

"Anyone hurt?" Simon asked.

"Not…recently."

"But there was an injury?" Laura asked. "Did you call 911?"

"Not yet."

"Who was hurt? How bad is it?"

"It's bad." Quinn's balding head shone under the lights. "The boat's propeller blade is fouled. On—on a body."

Simon was shocked into silence.

"Dead?" Laura demanded.

"Dead." A bead of sweat ran down Quinn's sideburns. "Really dead."

"Show me." She started across the room, her long stride hampered by her narrow skirt.

Simon kept pace beside her. Dealing with the body was her job. But this was his party, his property, his responsibility.

"Do you know who it is?" Laura asked Quinn as they made their way through the thinning crowd.

Quinn shook his head. "Once I realized… Once I saw what was caught in the motor, I got the guests off the boat and away from the dock. The pilot and I pulled him… We freed the prop blade. But his skin… The face…" He shuddered.

Really dead. Obviously decayed.

"Okay," Laura said gently. "I'll call dispatch to arrange transport for the body. And we'll need a coroner." She was already rummaging in her tiny bag for a cell phone. "You did a good job, Quinn. I've got it from here."

"Some party," Dylan said to Simon an hour later.

They stood on the path looking down on the dock. The wind had picked up. The temperature was dropping. Floodlights obliterated the twinkling strands in the trees, converting the festive setting to stark planes and sharp shadows. White-faced figures in dark windbreakers or khaki coveralls with orange stripes jumped and crawled over the scene.

A police boat and two private craft bumped for space alongside Simon's sleek cabin cruiser. The boat hired to transport guests to and from the marina was tethered to the other side, its propeller hidden from sight. Simon was queasily grateful.

"What are you doing here?" he asked Dylan. "Guests are restricted to the house."

"That's what I came to talk to you about. You still have almost fifty people here. Unless you figure out what to do with them, you're going to have either a riot or one hell of a pajama party on your hands."

Fifty people. Dear God.

"Tell Quinn to keep the bar open. See if the musicians will play another set. As soon as the police clear the way, we can start ferrying guests back in the cabin cruiser."

Dylan nodded. "Where's the dead guy?"

"On the police boat. They loaded the body ten minutes ago."

"And Laura?"

Simon jerked his chin toward the dock. "Down there."

She was talking to the woman in the orange slicker—the coroner, Simon thought. Laura's lavender dress was crumpled and soiled, her face white and set under the unforgiving lights, her shoulders covered by his tuxedo jacket.

Earlier, Simon had tried to go to her, only to be escorted firmly away by a uniformed patrolman. In the end, Simon had had to settle for the officer's promise to take her his jacket. Just because she had to work didn't mean she had to freeze.

Laura had slipped her arms into his jacket sleeves. For one moment, her gaze sought Simon's where he stood beneath the trees. For one moment, their eyes had met and clung. Connection flashed between them, bright and charged as a laser beam. And then she'd nodded once, in thanks or acknowledgment, and returned to her grim work.

She hadn't looked his way in quite a while. Beneath his oversize jacket, her shoulders stood up sharply. Simon watched as she finished her conversation with Orange Slicker and tensed in anticipation. She'd look up now. She'd come to him now.

She didn't.

Instead a lean, disciplined figure detached from the knot of men clustered near the police boat and climbed the hill with long, purposeful strides.

"Mr. Ford." The newcomer's voice was polite, his eyes sharp and cool as the wind off the lake.

"Simon." Simon stepped forward to shake hands. Had they met before? Where the hell was Laura? "My brother Dylan."

"Jarek Denko," the man offered, extending his hand to Dylan.

The police chief. Laura's boss. The man who had yanked her from his case for "conflict of interest."

"Are you almost done down there?" Simon asked. "I need to speak to Laura."

He could see her clambering on board the police boat, her movements as stiff as a much older woman's. Where did she think she was going?

"Detective Baker is accompanying the body to McCormick Mercy Hospital."

"Is that necessary?"

"Yes," Denko said simply. He looked at Dylan. "Could you give us a minute, sir?"

Dylan cocked an eyebrow. "You want me to go?" he asked his brother.

Simon was surprised and grateful Dylan would ask. "I need you at the house. Julie needs you," he added, when it seemed Dylan might still object. "I'll be along as soon as I can."

Dylan shrugged. "Fine. I'll go bribe the musicians."

Simon waited until his brother was out of earshot before he turned back to the police chief. "What is it? Or more precisely, who is it?"

"The body is being transported to the hospital morgue. The medical examiner will perform a complete autopsy and confirm ID."

"Confirm?"

Denko met his eyes. "The victim went into the water fully clothed and carrying identification."

Simon felt sick. "Who is it?"

But he already knew.

"The identification found with the body belongs to Peter Swirsky."

You understand I'm only doing this to clear my father.

Simon swore silently and glanced at the boat. Laura had ducked under the canopy to stand by the body, wrapped in yellow plastic on the deck. He couldn't see her face.

"How long has he been dead?"

"That's for the M.E. to say."

"That's a load of crap," Simon said. "How long has he been dead?"

"The body was in the water long enough for tissue decomposition to begin, which creates the gas that brought it to the surface. Eight to ten days, at a guess."

"Since the break in to my lab."

"That's right. When was the last time you saw Mr. Swirsky?"

Simon stiffened. He didn't remember. That night was still a blank to him. "Do I need a lawyer?"

Denko returned his gaze levelly. "Do you want a lawyer?"

"I want to know what happened." God, did he want to know. "How did he die?"

"I can't tell you that until after the autopsy report."

"But you must have some idea. You've seen the body. You have to know if he drowned or if he was shot or if he was hit over the head."

"Mr. Ford, you're not a pathologist. Neither am I. Without an autopsy to determine if there's sand or weed in the lungs, I won't know if he was alive when he went into the water or not. Between the natural abrasion that occurred while the body was at the bottom of the lake and the damage caused by the propeller, it's difficult to identify signs of a struggle. Is that clear?"

Horribly so.

That body down there, cut, abraded, decomposing, was Laura's father.

While Simon stood by, she had assisted in its grisly recovery from the water. She'd participated as the scene was photographed, sketched and inspected. She'd been there when the wallet was salvaged from her father's pocket, when the first tentative identification must have been made. She hadn't flinched, hadn't hesitated, hadn't once broken down.

Now she sat straight-backed in the prow of the boat, holding herself together, keeping herself apart. Competent. Contained. Alone.

It ripped him up inside.

"I have to see her," he said abruptly.

"Not now," Denko said.

He nearly snarled. "Do you think you can stop me?"

"I'm sure I can," Denko said evenly. "But it's not my decision."

Simon rounded on him, baffled and angry. "What are you talking about?"

"It's hers. She wants to do this herself. She asked me to tell you she'll be in touch."

Simon swore, turning to glare after the departing boat. It was leaving. She was actually leaving him.

"Aren't you going to ask about the rubies?" Denko asked behind him.

"What?"

He hadn't thought about the rubies. How could he think about rubies when Laura was leaving?

"Aren't you going to ask if the rubies were recovered with the body?"

"God, I hope not."

"Excuse me?" Denko's quiet, impassive voice was touched with surprise.

"Bad enough her father's dead. Worse for her if she has to accept he was a thief."

The other man was silent so long that Simon's hopes, never very high to begin with, sank. "You found them, didn't you?" he said flatly.

"Actually, no. We didn't."

Simon was relieved enough to feel annoyed. "So, what will you do now?"

"I'm assigning an officer to stay here tonight until we determine cause of death."

"Why?"

"I've got one dead body on my hands. I don't need another."

"And I don't need a baby-sitter. There are enough damn people on the island already."

"Detective Baker asked me to provide you with extra security," Denko said.

She'd thought of him. In the middle of her own shock and tragedy, she'd worried about his safety.

Simon might have been moved by that. He could even have hoped it was a sign she cared.

But there was a good chance Laura considered looking after him her job. Which meant she would attend to him whether she gave a damn or not.

"E.C.I.P. provided extra security for the party, and I've got Quinn. You want to make work for your officers, get someone to look after Laura."

"Detective Baker doesn't need a baby-sitter, either."

"She needs somebody." And she didn't want him. Hurt, anger and wounded male ego combined and reacted in his stomach. Well, he was just going to have to change her mind. But in the meantime… "She's taking her father to the morgue, for God's sake. She shouldn't be alone after that."

Denko regarded him thoughtfully. "I'll call home. My wife will want Laura to spend tonight at our house."

"She'll say no," Simon predicted.

Laura was good at saying no.

Jarek Denko smiled. "No one says no to Tess."

Laura sat upright, numb with shock and rigid with determination, as white water churned by the prow. The engine chugged. The wind fretted. Her blood buzzed in her ears.

She took deep, careful breaths so she wouldn't pass out, inhaling through her mouth, as if the smell of rot could permeate the plastic tarp in the stern and infect her. She didn't want to smell anything. She didn't want to feel anything.

Tightening her trembling hands in her lap, she concentrated on the rise and fall of the water. It was hard to grieve for the father who had turned his back on her. Dead or alive, hard-eyed, hard-handed Pete Swirsky had never encouraged signs of affection from his children.

But he had given her life and shaped it. And now he was dead.

Gusts lashed the prow, raising spray from the water that

lay like tears on her cheeks. Laura shivered, buffeted by guilt, chilled by a regret keener than the wind that she had never made her peace with her father.

"Cold?"

Kathy Cowan, the coroner, moved forward from the stern, her round face alight with sympathy. "Can I get you something? A blanket?"

"No, I'm…" *Fine.* The lie stuck in her throat. "Warm enough. Thanks."

Kathy patted her clasped hands. "Let me know if you change your mind." The doctor made her way, a little unsteadily, to the pilot's cabin.

Laura pulled Simon's jacket closer around her. The tang of him still clung to the material, hotly sexy, coolly expensive. On impulse, she rubbed her cheek against the collar and then cursed herself for her weakness. But there was no one to see. No one to recognize or report her foolish feminine behavior. Simon would never know how close she came, for one moment in the dark, to forgetting what she owed him and herself.

I need to solve this case. And you need someone to protect your ass.

She turned her face to the water. The wind stung tears to her eyes and then whipped them away.

Chapter 12

"Clean sheets are on the bed," Tess Denko said as she led Laura upstairs. "Clean towels in the bathroom. Jarek said he didn't give you much time to pack, so let me know if you need anything."

The police chief's wife was effortlessly, exotically beautiful, with thick dark hair and bright red nails and a casual female confidence that somehow survived being woken at almost two in the morning to welcome an unexpected house guest.

Laura felt like the little matchstick girl being foisted on the queen. She shivered and clutched Simon's jacket tighter.

"I'm sorry to put you out," she said stiffly.

"You're not putting anyone out," Tess assured her, opening a door. "Allie's at a sleepover, so you're in her room tonight. I hope that's all right."

Allie was the chief's twelve-year-daughter. Exhausted,

Laura looked around the blue bedroom, sponge painted with clouds and decorated with rock posters, and felt more out-of-place than ever. "It's great. Thanks."

The white twin bed was piled with pillows and stuffed animals. She wanted to crawl under the covers, pull them over her head and not come up for a week.

"Well." Tess studied her, her warm golden eyes concerned. "That door's the baby's room. The bathroom is there. We're just across the hall. Are you sure you're going to be all right?"

Laura dredged up a smile. She was not going to lose it in front of her chief's wife. "I'm good. Thanks."

"Okay." Tess ambushed her with a hug.

Laura didn't do hugs, but the other woman's generous sympathy brought unwanted tears to her eyes.

"Sleep tight," Tess said. "We'll see you in the morning."

Mortified, Laura stepped back, her throat tight, and nodded.

Standing in the middle of the blue carpet, she listened as the other woman's footsteps crossed the hall. She heard a door open, a male murmur and Tess's soft reply. The overheard exchange made Laura vaguely uncomfortable. As a boss and as a man, Jarek Denko kept his private life private. This intimate glimpse of his other side left her feeling disoriented and even more alone.

Mechanically, she undressed, folding Simon's jacket neatly to lay across the foot of the bed, letting her dress slither in a heap to the floor, and unhooking the Iron Maiden push-up bra. Wearing only her panties, she crawled under the covers. She was drained, empty, shaking with exhaustion and the hard, cold aftershocks of loss. But sleep did not come.

Finally she reached down and dragged Simon's jacket from the bottom of the bed. She crushed it to her face, breathing in his faint, unmistakable scent. Hugging the jacket like a security blanket, she drifted at last into uneasy sleep.

* * *

She woke to the sound of crying.

Laura bolted from her pillow and stared blearily at the clock: 9:27. Her day had just started, and she was already behind. She had calls to make. Things to do. All the obligations that attended an unexpected death pressed in on her.

Simon's jacket lay creased under her. She tried to shake the wrinkles out, but the task was hopeless.

Julie's words came back to her. *You can count on him to rescue you when things are really dire.*

Laura's breathing hitched. This was pretty dire.

But she couldn't function as a police officer if she hung around waiting for rescue. She couldn't function, period. She could grow to depend on him, and then where would they be? What would she do when he didn't need her anymore, when he got back his life and his memory and didn't want her anymore? She stuffed the jacket in her bag to deal with later and dug out jeans and a T-shirt.

While she was dressing, the crying stopped. The baby, she guessed. She scuttled across the hall to brush her teeth and swipe at her hair, praying she wouldn't run into her boss before she'd made herself presentable.

But the hallway was quiet. Empty.

The aroma of coffee floated up the stairs. Laura almost whimpered as she followed it down and into the kitchen.

One cup, she promised herself. As soon as she was fueled for the day, as soon as she had enough caffeine in her system to function, she would go.

Tess took one look at her face and reached for the coffeepot. She poured Laura's coffee, holding the pot away from the dark-haired baby on her hip.

"Hot," Tess said firmly and set the mug on the kitchen table, out of his reach.

Laura gulped gratefully. "Thanks."

Tess, mercifully, didn't seem to feel the need for conversation before coffee. Laura had downed half a mug before she realized her hostess was in full makeup and a black linen dress.

"Gee." Laura cleared her throat. "I didn't know I should dress up for breakfast."

Tess grinned. "Mass this morning," she explained. "Jarek went to pick up Allie, so you'll actually have some peace and quiet around here."

Her protest was automatic. "Oh, I couldn't—"

"Can you hold him?" Tess thrust her son at Laura. "I have to run upstairs for my shoes."

"Hold…?"

"Nicholas."

Laura regarded the baby with misgiving. She didn't back down from bar fights, vehicle stops or drunken domestic disputes. But babies scared the living daylights out of her. She hadn't thought about babies—she hadn't let herself think about babies—in years.

Since she'd lost her own. A pang lodged under her heart.

"I don't know," she said, "I…"

A car engine rumbled in the driveway.

"Oh, Lord, there's the car," Tess said, distracted. "I'll be right back."

She dumped her baby on Laura's lap and dashed for the stairs.

Laura blinked, her hands moving automatically to support the child.

Nicholas blinked back, clearly as uncertain as she was about this new development.

Laura cleared her throat. "Okay, here's the deal. I won't scream if you don't."

His face creased.

Panicked, she rushed into speech. "Is that a problem for you? Because I understand you probably have a tough time communicating at this point. So if I screw up, like if I'm holding you wrong or something, it's okay if you let me know."

Nicholas gurgled.

"That's good, right?"

He flailed his baby hands and pushed with his baby feet against her thighs.

Encouraged, Laura bounced him tentatively on her lap.

The doorbell rang. She ignored it. Maybe she hadn't dropped him yet, but there was no way she was going to try to walk and hold the baby at the same time. Besides, she figured Jarek could let himself into his own house.

She heard Tess coming down the stairs and the door open.

Hey, she wanted to call, don't forget about us.

But then Nicholas reached for her coffee mug and she lunged to move it out of his way.

"Oh, no, you don't. Hot," Laura said firmly, doing her best to imitate Tess.

Nicholas showed his gums in a gap mouthed, happy smile.

Her own lips curved. "Don't give me that look. I'm a police officer. We're enforcing the rules until your mother gets back."

He continued to grin, clearly delighted with himself and pleased with her.

Laura couldn't help herself. She grinned back and bent to nuzzle his neck, inhaling his sweet baby scent. He chortled and kicked.

"Visitor for you," Tess announced from the kitchen door.

Laura straightened fast enough to give herself whiplash. Tess was beaming. And behind her...

Simon.

Their eyes met. Held. In Laura's whole life, nobody had ever looked at her the way Simon did, as if she was a puzzle he desperately needed to solve or the answer to a question he didn't know how to ask.

Her tongue dried to the roof of her mouth. Her blood drummed in her ears. "I, uh…"

"Did great," Tess interrupted her. "Thanks."

She swooped up her gurgling son and balanced him competently on her hip. "Gotta run. Jarek and Allie are waiting in the car. Key to the front door is on the mantel if you want to go out for, well…" Her bright reporter's gaze traveled over Simon. "Anything. Take care."

She dashed out, leaving Simon and an awkward silence behind.

Laura wanted to run to him. Or duck under the table to hide.

Since either action seemed incredibly stupid, she stuck where she was, gripping her coffee mug.

"How are you?" he asked quietly, not moving from the door.

"I'm okay." She risked another look. His face was pale. His eyes were serious. Her insides jangled with yearning, nerves and coffee. "How are you?"

He frowned. "Fine. I'm sorry about your father."

Her throat closed. She swallowed hard. "Thank you."

"I didn't get a chance to tell you last night."

The faint rebuke in his voice made her flush. "No. Sorry. Your jacket is upstairs. I was going to have it dry-cleaned."

"I didn't come to get my jacket, Laura."

The heat deepened in her cheeks. She plowed on. "The autopsy is scheduled for ten tomorrow morning. From the look of things, he—the body went into the water eight to ten days ago. Once the medical examiner finishes his report, we should have a clearer picture of what happened the night you were attacked."

He paced toward her. "I didn't come to talk about the case, either."

How could she put the necessary distance between them when he stood so close? She took a deep breath. "Why did you come?"

He stopped, his eyebrows raising. "I came to be with you. People need to be notified. Arrangements made. I thought you could use some help."

"You want to help me," she repeated carefully.

"Why not?"

For a smart man, he could be amazingly dense at times. She'd been thinking about this over and over until she was sick of it. Until she was sick, period. "Because my father isn't missing anymore. He didn't go on vacation. He didn't disappear. He's dead. And there's a very real chance he's guilty."

"There was always the possibility he was guilty," Simon said.

She shot him a resentful look. "Thanks. Now I feel lots better."

"The only thing that's changed is now there's a possibility I killed him."

She'd thought of that. It shook her to realize he had, too. "You can't have. You were unconscious."

"You only have my word for that."

"And the bump on your head. There's no way you could self-inflict a wound that size at that angle."

"We could have fought."

She didn't want to talk about it. She didn't even want to think about it. But she couldn't let Simon blame himself for a tragedy that wasn't his fault. She had to deal with his fears. They both did.

"Sorry to burst your macho illusions, Ford, but you didn't fight. There were no signs of a struggle. You were in the lab. My father was in the lake. Unless you dragged his body while you were unconscious, you didn't put him there."

"I was the last person to see him alive."

"The last person we know of."

Simon's face was set, his eyes tormented. "Did E.C.I.P. deliver the printout of the computer log yet?"

A great wave of pity and reluctance moved through Laura. She bit her lip. "Palmer has it."

"And?"

Damn the man's persistence. "All right," she admitted. "According to the log, the only people to access the lab that night were you and my father. That doesn't prove you were the only people there."

"No, but it's a damn good clue."

"Anyone inside the lab could have opened the door to admit someone else."

"So you think I opened the door to your father's killer? Or did he open the door himself?"

"We don't know yet that he was killed."

"We don't know that he wasn't."

She rubbed her forehead, as if that could force some new idea into her tired brain. "He could have slipped and fallen making his escape."

"But then the rubies would have been found on his body."

She glared at him. Was he *trying* to be charged with her father's murder? "Maybe he had an accomplice. Once he was inside the lab, he could have let someone else in. Or you could have."

Simon's eyebrows raised. "So the accomplice killed him, took the stones and disposed of his body."

It wasn't a terrible idea.

"I don't know," Laura said. "I'm waiting on the autopsy results. But it's one explanation."

A slight smile touched his lips. His eyes were dark and unreadable. "Why are you so determined to prove I'm innocent?"

Her heart filled. The words trembled behind her stubbornly set mouth. *Because I care about you, you stupid moron.*

She angled her jaw. "Why are you so determined to prove you're guilty?"

His smile broadened. "Good question. All right, Detective. Let's see if we can't form a hypothesis that satisfies us both." He paced the kitchen. "Let's start with the one obvious fact we've overlooked. Your father was the security guard that night. Maybe he interrupted the robbery. Maybe whoever attacked me murdered him."

Hope and fear lodged together in Laura's chest, making it hard to breathe. She wanted to believe her father was innocent. In her heart of hearts, she did believe it. But…satisfied? Dear God, no. Because if Simon's theory was right, he was in even more danger. If his theory was right, her father's killer was still out there. And an attacker who killed once would be more likely to kill again.

"In that case, there should have been signs of a struggle."

"Maybe your father apprehended him outside the lab. Or down at the dock."

It was possible. Even plausible, Laura thought with rising hope.

"So do we have a motive for this mystery attacker?"

Simon sat on the edge of the kitchen table. "Half a million dollars in cultured gemstones seems sufficient motive. Not to mention notebooks, papers, whatever else I kept in the safe."

Laura frowned. "Somebody still had to let the thief in."

"Not necessarily. Was your father's passcard recovered with his body?"

She didn't know. She hadn't asked. Her failure shook her. "I… His personal effects should be returned to me tomorrow. I can ask."

Simon's eyes were sharp and cool. "Ask when the cards were used, too."

"The chief might not tell me. Would it make a difference?"

"It might."

She shook her head. "Maybe it's a good thing I'm off the case. Maybe I am too close to see clearly."

"And maybe you're the only one close enough to see at all. You'll figure it out," he said.

She didn't deserve his confidence. She was terrified of making another mistake.

"I'm not sure I want to."

"You said you wanted the truth," he reminded her gently. He brushed his fingers down her cheek. She fought the temptation to close her eyes and lean into his touch. "Whatever it is, you'll handle it."

"Yeah." She sighed and pulled away. "I'm good at handling things."

Simon's hand dropped. "You are." Annoyance edged his voice. "It would, however, be helpful if you occasionally realized you don't need to handle everything alone."

Startled, she met his eyes. Beneath the simmering temper was real hurt. She hadn't wanted to hurt him. She hadn't realized she could.

She depended on her fellow cops for backup, just as they depended on her. But nobody at work expected her to holler for help in a situation she had under control. Nobody in her life wanted to hear about her problems. Or share them. Simon's insistence on doing both made her feel odd. Special.

Threatened.

"If this is about last night," she said carefully, "I was only doing my job."

"I'm not stopping you from doing your job. But I'd like to help you get through the rest of it."

"Why?" she asked baldly.

He hesitated.

Her heart pounded. What did she expect him to say? *Because, my darling Laura, I love you truly, madly, deeply and I want to be there for you always.* Yeah, like that would ever happen.

"You helped me," he said finally. "I owe you."

Fair enough, she thought, squashing her disappointment.

"You don't owe me anything. I helped you because I wanted to."

"Then let me do the same."

She turned her mug in her hands. "I don't even know where to begin," she confessed. "My father and I weren't… close. I don't know what he would have wanted. I don't even know if he had a lawyer. It was different when…"

When Tommy died.

The memory of her young husband's flag-draped coffin shivered through her, haunting as the bright notes of the trumpet over his grave. Maybe he hadn't been the great love of her life. Maybe she hadn't been his. But he'd been willing to marry her, and that counted for something. It counted for a lot, actually.

"Different when it was your husband," Simon said, his eyes watchful.

She nodded, embarrassed by her show of emotion and grateful for his understanding. "Tommy was navy. The navy takes care of its own."

"So do I," Simon said.

She gaped at him.

"He did work for me," Simon said blandly. "Your father."

Heat washed over her. "Oh."

Right. Of course. He didn't mean… He didn't want…

Simon pulled a slim, silver electronic notebook with a matching stylus from his pocket. "The autopsy's tomorrow, you said. When will they release the body?"

"Tuesday, probably." She watched him jot on the tiny screen, feeling as though she'd landed on the wrong side of an interview.

"Church?" Simon asked.

Laura summoned her thoughts to respond. "I don't think so. My father wasn't a churchgoing man. Not since…" Unexpectedly her throat closed. Jeez, she was weepy. She took a gulp of coffee, annoyed with herself. "Not since my mother died. I could check and see if he was registered anywhere in the diocese."

"Later." He made another note. "Unless you have another preference, I thought we'd let Carolyn investigate funeral homes. Of course, the final decision will be yours."

"Wait a minute." Amused, astounded, she looked down at his elegant gadget and then up into his eyes. "Are you making notes for my father's funeral on your PDA?"

He met her gaze evenly. A muscle twitched in his jaw. "Yes. Any objections?"

"No, it's very…" Logical. Methodical. Typical. She smiled. "Very practical," she said.

His expression remained blank, a smooth shield against criticism. "I am practical."

Okay, she'd pushed the wrong button somewhere. "Is that a problem for you?"

Just for a moment, his eyes communicated for him. She saw his uncertainty, his longing, his need. But she didn't know what caused them.

"Not really," he returned coolly. "Is it a problem for you?"

It had obviously been a problem for somebody. Laura tried to imagine Simon as a thoughtful, solitary boy growing up with a profligate father and a succession of stepmothers. Had they taught him to hide his feelings?

Or, compared to the emotionally extravagant adults in his life, had he sometimes felt he didn't have any?

Impulsively she reached out and covered his hand with hers. "Nope. I'm not what you'd call touchy-feely, either."

He turned his hand over and threaded his fingers with hers. "Maybe we could work on that. We could be good for each other."

He was wrong, but she left her hand in his anyway, because it felt so good. "I doubt it. If you hadn't gotten conked on the head, you wouldn't give me the time of day."

"And you wouldn't speak to me except to write me a traffic ticket."

"See? We're relationship challenged. It's like the blind leading the blind. The lame supporting the lame. The romantically impaired giving advice to the emotionally stunted."

His eyebrows arched. She couldn't tell if he was offended or amused. "Which one am I?"

"Take your pick."

He considered. "What if I don't like your choices?"

She shrugged. "Then you make changes, I guess. It's not too late for you."

His eyes were steady on her face. "Not too late for either of us."

Her throat felt tight. "It is for me. I won't ever… I can't ever…"

Her voice shook with unshed tears. Damn it.

"He loved you, you know," Simon volunteered unexpectedly.

"What?"

"Your father. He loved you."

"Right." She swallowed hard. "That's why he didn't talk to me for ten years."

"That's why he kept a picture of you in his bedroom. He was trying to hold on to the little girl he loved. He didn't know how to say it, he didn't know how to show it, but he loved you, Laura."

Terrific, she thought. This was a hell of a time to discover she made a habit of falling for men who couldn't express their feelings.

Still, it comforted her to think maybe her father had thought of her sometimes with affection, had remembered her sometimes with love.

She cleared her throat; squeezed Simon's hand. "Thanks."

"It's nothing," he said gruffly. He looked down at the PDA. "Now, about the newspaper announcement…"

Okay, so it wasn't a declaration of love, Laura thought. But it was help, and she was grateful.

Thirty minutes later, Simon flipped the cover shut on his electronic notebook.

"That's it. E.C.I.P. should have most of the information in your father's personnel file. Have you spoken with your brother yet?"

Laura shifted uncomfortably on her chair. "I was waiting until after the autopsy."

"Why?"

"The M.E. hasn't made an official identification of the body."

"Do you really think that's someone else in the morgue?" Simon asked.

"Not exactly," she muttered.

"Then why the delay? Exactly."

She scowled. "My brother's not answering his phone."

"You've tried to call?"

Will you call your brother? he'd asked as they left her father's apartment.

I don't need you to tell me how to do my job.

She flushed. "Yes. He hasn't returned any of my messages."

"Have you tried calling him at work?"

She didn't know where he worked or what he did, really. Something administrative. Their father had gotten him the job the Chicago way—through connections. Paul complained sometimes about the dreary routine, the dead end pay, the superior macho attitudes of some of his co-workers. But despite Laura's urging, he had never moved on.

"Then maybe he was busy," Simon said.

"Uh-huh. And maybe he has caller ID and he's avoiding me."

"Then he won't recognize this number," Simon pointed out logically.

She took a sip of cold coffee, the taste bitter in her mouth. Stalling. "Even if Paul picks up, there's no guarantee he'll want to talk to me."

"You can still talk to him. You need to tell him about your father."

She hunched her shoulders. "Yeah, 'Hi, Paul, Daddy's dead' is a hell of an icebreaker."

But she could not ignore her duty. Picking up the wall phone, she punched in her brother's number from memory.

He answered on the fourth ring, his voice gravelly with sleep or smoke. "'Lo?"

"Paul?" Her voice sounded shaky. Uncertain. She took another deep breath and tried again. "It's Laura."

"Where are you calling from?"

Her heart sank. He was avoiding her. Or were grief and fatigue on top of her usual cop's paranoia making her imagine things? She was very aware of Simon, still sitting at the table, watching her. "I'm at a friend's."

"What do you want?"

"I have bad news."

"That used to be my line," Paul observed. "Are you in trouble?"

Laura's heart quailed. How many times had she asked him that question, with just that inflection of exasperated concern in her voice? After their mother's death, her brother's rebellious streak coupled with the hard-line discipline at home had pushed him to make bad friends and bad choices. Their house had reverberated with the rumbles of failing grades and detentions, street fights and school suspensions. Laura had learned to dread the notes from teachers, the middle-of-the-night phone calls, the constant battles with their father, afraid that each new transgression would be the one that drove her brother from the house.

But in the end, it had been Laura who left and Paul who stayed. What would their father's death mean to him?

She turned to face the wall. Lowered her voice. "There's been an accident."

"What do you mean, an accident? Are you hurt?"

Simon's chair scraped back from the kitchen table. She heard him cross the table, felt him stand behind her. "I'm fine. But the police recovered a body from the lake last night. Here in Eden."

"So?"

Laura forced herself to continue. "Dad came up here about a week ago. On the Lumen Corp job."

"Dad's on vacation," Paul said.

She closed her eyes. "No. No, he's not."

"You are freaking kidding me."

"He's missing, Paul. He hasn't been in to work. And the body… The body that was recovered…"

"No," Paul said more forcibly.

"I'm sorry," Laura said helplessly.

Sorry he was dead. Sorry she had to be the one to tell him so. Sorry for leaving home, for leaving Paul to bear the brunt of their father's strictures and displeasure alone.

"It's not him," Paul said. "It can't be. He's on vacation."

"The medical examiner hasn't made a formal identification of the body yet," Laura said. "But—"

"Why don't you identify the body, if it's him?" Paul interrupted.

Laura swallowed. "I can't."

"Why not? You're still next of kin. Like it or not."

"I can't." She drew in a deep breath. "Nobody could. Pauly, he's... It's been ten days."

"Oh, Jesus." Her brother began to cry, horrible, muffled sounds made more terrible by distance.

Laura's knuckles turned white on the receiver. "I'm sorry," she said again, over and over. "I'm so sorry."

Simon watched and wanted to punch something.

Unfortunately, taking a swing at the police chief's kitchen cabinets wasn't going to help Laura. She'd demonstrated an irritating tendency to fight her own battles anyway.

She had turned her back on him. Her shoulders were braced. Her back tensed. She gripped the receiver like the handle of a club. Yet her voice was soft and controlled as she spoke to her brother, murmuring, explaining, consoling.

Simon wanted to make things better somehow. That's what he was good at, wasn't it? Solving problems. Figuring solutions. Fixing things.

He was uneasily aware that a woman's heart might be harder to calculate than a chemical formula or an angle of refraction. But he'd learned in the lab that most problems could be solved by patience and application.

He was willing to use both with Laura.

"...decide after I talk with the funeral director," she was saying. "He must have a suit in his closet. I'll see if the super will let me into his apartment."

The building super would let her do whatever she damn well wanted. Simon would make sure of it.

"No, you don't have to... A key?" The new note in Laura's voice plucked at Simon's attention. "Okay. Yeah. You could do that. I'll call you. Give me your number at work." She wrote something down. "No, of course I... Paul?"

Simon waited.

A long silence.

Laura cradled the phone, her hand lingering on the receiver. Her shoulders slumped. But when she turned to face Simon, her face was composed. "He hung up," she explained.

"Son of a bitch."

Her chin stuck out. "This is a difficult time for him."

"It's a difficult time for you, too." He didn't like the bright, blank look in her eyes. "Come here."

She jerked back. "No, I... You have to go."

"I'm not going anywhere," Simon said firmly, surprised to find he meant it. "Unless you're coming with me."

It wasn't too late for him, she'd said. He could change. He had changed.

Laura straightened her spine. "Fine," she said, clearly humoring him. "I need a ride back to my apartment."

"I can give you a ride."

But not, he decided, back to her apartment. She needed to get out. She needed to get away. She needed to let go. She needed room and time to grieve, to breathe, to be.

And he needed to be the one who gave them to her.

But he wouldn't argue with her now, he thought, observing the lines that dug around her mouth, the fatigue that lay like bruises under her eyes. She had too many decisions pressing in on her already and more than enough stress.

Patience and application, he thought again. He wouldn't badger her.

He'd kidnap her instead.

Chapter 13

Laura roused against the cream leather upholstery of Simon's Mercedes. "This isn't the way to my apartment."

"No," he agreed.

He should have figured she wouldn't let him get as far as the dock before she said something. Not a Stepford, his Laura. But he wished this once she'd sit back, shut up and let him take care of her.

She leaned forward to look out the windshield as he turned right on Harbor Street. "Turn left up here. Left. What are you doing?"

It didn't take a genius to see she was jittery and exhausted, subsisting on nerves and caffeine. He was no expert on women, but he understood cause and effect. He pulled to the curb in front of the Rose Farms Café.

Laura's eyes narrowed in annoyance. "Now what?"

"This will only take a minute," he promised and got out of the car.

It took three.

Simon slid back behind the wheel and tossed a white paper sack in her lap, relieved she hadn't left him flat.

"What's this?"

"Breakfast."

"I don't need..." Laura sniffed. "Did you get muffins?"

He smiled. "Why don't you open the bag and see?"

But she already had, with the single-minded concentration of a child ripping into presents on Christmas morning. Pleasure warmed him. He'd been right, after all. Maybe he was generally unperceptive, unfeeling, cold, but he'd been able to guess what she needed.

And if he was right about the muffins, his libido suggested slyly, maybe he was right about other things.

"Blueberry," Laura announced with satisfaction. "Lemon poppyseed, carrot, chocolate chip... Jeez, Ford, what did you do, buy out the store?"

Simon continued north on Harbor Street, seasonally crowded with locals hauling boat trailers and vacationing families in SUVs.

"One of each," he said, uncertain again. Defensive. "I didn't know what you like."

"One of everything is a nice start." She peeled back the paper from a blueberry muffin and bit into it. "God, this is good."

He glanced at her, the flush along her cheekbones, the crumb at the corner of her wide, mobile mouth and a hum kicked up in his blood. Patience, he reminded himself.

She swallowed and licked away the crumb. "I suppose you think you're pretty smart."

"I'm a genius," he said calmly, surprising a laugh from her.

"Yeah, I guess you are." She leaned across the gearshift,

straining against her shoulder strap to brush warm lips against his cheek. "A really sweet genius. Get any coffee?"

His body jumped. He inhaled sharply. Exhaled slowly. She was thanking him for breakfast, not inviting him to have sex, this wasn't about sex, this was about…

He made the mistake of looking at her again. She was watching him, her eyes direct and expectant, and he fell into her gaze and lost his train of thought.

"Hello? Coffee?" she prompted.

He wrenched his attention back to the road. They were lucky he hadn't driven up on the curb.

"Bottom of the bag," he said hoarsely. "Juice. It's better for you."

"Maybe I don't want what's good for me," she muttered, but she dug into the bag.

Simon clutched the wheel and tried hard not to think about all the things he could give her that wouldn't be good for her right now.

Laura popped the cap on her orange juice. "Where are we going?"

Simon detoured around a truck attempting to parallel park in front of a bait and tackle shop and turned right on Front Street. A strip of grass separated the road from the boardwalk. The sun beat down on glossy white hulls and weathered gray wood, on the bright sails and sparkling water.

"My boat's berthed here."

Laura lowered her juice bottle. "So?"

He pulled into his reserved spot in the marina parking lot. "It's a nice afternoon to go out on the water."

He saw the temptation and then the denial flash across her face. "I can't. I've got things to do."

"You've done enough." Strolling around the car, he opened the passenger side door. "Anyway, I wasn't inviting you."

She got out and crossed her arms against her chest. "So, you're dumping me here?"

"No." He grinned down at her indignant face. "I'm kidnapping you."

Sheer surprise kept her still long enough for him to retrieve the muffins and lock the car.

"Kidnapping is a Class 2 felony," she informed him.

But the spark returned to her eyes, the spark that had been missing before. Humor. Anticipation. He'd put it there. The knowledge made him feel proud, and humble, too. She was so beautiful with her strained face and shining eyes, and he was desperately afraid he was going to screw up.

He guided her toward the dock with a touch on her back, careful not to do anything that might spook her. "I'll take my chances."

She jumped easily onto the deck, ignoring his helping hand. "Guess I'll do the same. Do you remember how to pilot this thing?"

He freed the lines and followed her aboard. "It's coming back to me."

Laura tucked her hands into her back pockets, the pose creating some interesting body angles. "I'm glad."

He looked from her breasts to her eyes. "So am I."

Restlessly she strolled toward the cockpit. "You need any help?"

It pleased him she would offer. Pleased him to say no. He admired her tendency to take action and her confidence in taking charge. And admitted, to himself at least, that both pushed him to test her control. Egotistical bastard.

Positioning himself at the helm, he nodded to the curved companion bench. "Why don't you sit down? Relax."

Laura sat.

She didn't relax.

Not until they were away from the marina, the barking dogs, the shrieking kids, the Sunday fishermen, the flags and awnings of the waterfront. The twin engines putted past the buoy markers before throbbing to life. The bank slipped away, green and gold in the sunlight, and took her worries with it. The lake dashed on them, gray and white. A gull hung in the air behind the boat and then wheeled away.

Laura closed her eyes and let the wind lift her hair and her spirits.

It's a nice afternoon to go out on the water.

Yes.

When was the last time she used a day off to do anything besides catch up on paperwork and laundry? She couldn't even remember. Ever since Tommy died, she'd been focused on making something of herself. On proving something to herself or to her boss or to the cops she worked with. There hadn't been time for dates or distractions or simple pleasures. She tilted her head back, accepting the gift of the sun, letting it soak her brain and bake her shoulders.

The tenor of the engines changed. The boat quivered and slowed. Laura opened her eyes. They were already at the island.

She squelched her disappointment. "Your approach is off," she called. "You'll miss the dock."

Simon's lean, dark figure was silhouetted against the glass of the cockpit. He didn't even turn his head. "I'm not aiming for the dock."

Fine by her. She'd spent too much time crawling over those planks last night, cataloging, photographing, searching for evidence.

She struggled to sit up on the narrow, padded bench. "Is there another way to the house?"

Simon guided the cabin cruiser expertly along the shore.

Trees bowed over the water, casting deep shadow and bright reflections. "Not unless we make a swim for it."

She frowned. "Then, why…?"

"Dylan is staying at the house. And Julie." Simon glanced over his shoulder. "Even if you were in any shape to face them, I'd prefer to have you to myself for a while."

She could face anything. But…

I'd prefer to have you to myself for a while.

Her heart beat faster.

The boat nosed into a quiet inlet, where the rocks stretched out protecting arms to cradle a bowl of smooth, dark water. Trees shielded the view on three sides. Lake and sky bounded the fourth. Sun poured over the boat like honey, sticky and golden.

Simon dropped anchor and cut the engines. The sudden silence pressed down like a change in air pressure, making it hard to breathe.

He stepped away from the controls and stripped his shirt over his head.

Laura gawked. He had a man's body, hard and lean, with broad shoulders and well-developed biceps. He didn't look like any science nerd she'd known in high school.

He turned to face her, revealing flat brown nipples and an intriguing line of hair that ran over his abdomen and disappeared into his pants. Her throat went dry.

"What are you doing?" she croaked.

He raised one eyebrow. "It's hot."

Yeah, it was. Despite the faint breeze that stirred the trees and ruffled the water out on the lake, the sheltered cove was definitely warm. And staring at Simon Ford's half-naked body wasn't doing a darn thing to cool things off.

Laura licked her lips. "So?"

"I'm going in for a swim. Want to join me?"

She gestured to her jeans. "I'm not dressed for swimming."

His eyes glinted. "You could get undressed."

Her heart thumped. "We have statutes against public nudity."

"We're not in public. This is a private beach."

She tossed her hair over her shoulders. "I'm still too old to go skinny dipping."

"Suit yourself," he said easily, and dropped his pants.

Laura sucked in her breath. She was a cop. She'd been propositioned from the back of her squad car, chased perverts through the park, been mooned by high school kids out of car windows. The unexpected sight of male body parts did not send her into palpitations like the virginal heroine of a romance novel.

On the other hand, none of those males had had bodies as fine as Simon Ford's.

She exhaled. "I thought you were a briefs kind of guy."

"Boxers."

"Yeah, I can see that."

Along with a lot—a whole lot—more. Her gaze traveled from his hard chest shadowed with hair down to lean, powerful thighs, muscled calves, big feet. Heat spread and coiled in her belly.

She jerked her eyes to his face. He smiled at her lazily. He knew exactly what effect he had on her. Bastard.

"Sure I can't tempt you?"

Her heart pounded. The air was thick enough to choke on.

"To swim," she said, feeling her way.

He nodded, his eyes never leaving hers. "If you're up for it."

It was a challenge. A dare. This kind of dare she could handle.

She grinned fiercely and got to her feet. "You're on."

Maybe she wasn't model thin or stripper lush. But she took pride in her well-toned, disciplined body. On this battle-ground, at least, she was a match for him. She tugged her T-shirt up and off. She unzipped her jeans and wiggled them over her hips.

Take that, Mr. Cool Science Guy, she thought, and kicked her jeans across the deck.

Simon's eyes flared.

Her underwear was pale blue cotton. Basic. Boring. Cut high on the thigh, it provided as much coverage as a bathing suit. But even though it wasn't especially revealing, it sent the right message. She hoped. *Here I am, take it or leave it.*

She stood before him, shivering with nerves and lust. *Take me.*

Without a word, Simon walked past her to the swim plat-form at the back of the boat and dived cleanly into the cool, dark water.

Screw you, Laura thought, astonished.

Except apparently she wasn't going to get the opportunity.

Well. She thought about that as she watched Simon pull away from the boat, cutting through the water with the easy breathing and long, powerful strokes of an experienced swim-mer. At least she knew now how he kept that amazing body in shape.

She knew very little else. She could only guess at his feel-ings. She wasn't even sure of her own.

Scowling, she sat on the edge of the platform and dangled her pale legs in the water. It was cold. Her toes curled.

What did she want from him, anyway?

His voice came back to her. *What do you want? Promises?*

And her reply: *This isn't about what I want from you. It's about what I expect of myself.*

She watched Simon strike out for open water with strong, confident strokes and realized she wanted more than comfort or an afternoon's escape. More than duty and rigid adherence to someone else's rule book. More than she'd allowed herself to have or imagined she deserved.

She wanted to dare and dream again, the way she hadn't since she got knocked up at seventeen. To take a risk that wasn't calculated. To live a little larger than life.

She wanted hope. Intimacy. Passion. And she wanted them all with Simon.

Now all she had to do was persuade him to give them to her.

She jumped into the water. And shrieked as the water closed over her head.

My God, it was cold.

She kicked for the surface, flailing around to warm up, figuring sooner or later she'd get feeling back in her extremities, when Simon's hard, warm hands grabbed her shoulders and hauled her close to his body.

"What's the matter? Are you hurt? Do you have a cramp?" Water spiked his eyelashes. Concern filled his voice. Which would have been great—he had beautiful eyes and she loved his concern—except she felt like a damn fool.

"No, I, uh…" She struggled to right herself in the water.

He thrust a hairy, muscular thigh between her legs to support her, pulling her closer with one arm. *Hello.*

She flushed. "I was cold, that's all."

Their bodies nudged together. Drifted apart.

He squinted at her. "You were cold."

"Yeah. In case you haven't noticed, the water's freezing."

"I noticed," he assured her. "It's a guy thing."

Her laugh bubbled up, surprising them both.

He loosened his hold on her waist. Their legs brushed underwater. "You sure you're all right?"

She nodded, both more relaxed and more keyed up than she could remember being in her life. "Sorry about the scream."

He smiled wryly. "Me, too. I was hoping I could practice my life saving skills."

Her heart zinged. But before she could respond, he released her. His shoulders bunched as he hauled himself up on the boat's platform. Water streamed from his hair, glistened on his chest, dripped down that intriguing line of hair. His wet shorts molded to his body.

Laura sucked in her breath and nearly choked.

"Hey." He leaned over and offered her a hand.

She didn't need help. Pretending she did seemed hypocritical. Conniving had never been her style. But in this case, Laura figured, a little hand-to-hand contact was worth it. Grabbing his wrist, she let him hoist her up. He was breathing hard. So was she. Now, she thought, as they stood there, practically naked and dripping wet, her heart beating faster, his eyes dark and surprised, the air around them charged like the lake before a summer storm.

Now.

Simon shook his head slightly and stepped back. "I'll get some towels. You need to warm up."

She was warm. Hell, she was hot. She practically steamed.

Confused, disappointed, Laura watched him walk toward the forward cabin door. Okay, conniving wasn't working. She'd have to go with direct.

"Was it something I said?" she yelled.

Simon turned around, keeping his distance. "What are you talking about?"

She opened her arms, disgusted with them both, the romantically impaired and relationship challenged. "This. Us. Look at me." Her panties were almost transparent. Her nipples stood out, bold exclamations of sex, against the material of her bra.

"I see you," Simon said quietly.

Which would have been totally embarrassing except it was clear—it was *really* clear, his wet boxers gloved his arousal, his eyes were hard and dark—that he liked what he saw.

Laura expelled her breath in frustration. "I'm available. You're interested. So what's the deal?"

Simon's body was taut. He did not move. "I don't want to take advantage."

"Of the situation?"

His eyes were serious, searching, the pupils dilated. "Of you."

A great surge of relief washed through her. He wasn't rejecting her. He was being considerate. The dumbass.

"Guess it's up to me, then," she grumbled. "Why do women always have to do all the work?"

And she jumped him. Literally.

She felt his body brace to absorb her assault, felt him harden with shock and then with need. Thank God.

Twining her arms around his neck, she planted a kiss full on his mouth. His arms rose automatically to hold her. His arousal pressed instinctively against her belly. Laura smiled against his mouth, loving the way his water-cooled skin heated at contact, the way his body adjusted to hers, angles to planes, bumps to hollows.

She kissed him again, longer this time, putting her heart and her soul and some tongue into it. He kissed her back, his hand coming up to mold her breast, the rasp of damp cotton against her nipple a pleasure-pain so intense she moaned. His touch gentled instantly, tracing light, dizzying circles through the wet barrier of cloth.

It was too much. It wasn't nearly enough. She reached for her bra, but Simon was ahead of her, flicking open the clasp, peeling back the cup, exposing her damp breast to the soft caress of the air.

"Beautiful," he murmured.

And Laura, previously bold, was suddenly, shyly self-conscious. She tugged at him as if she could cover herself with his body. He caught her hands, holding them away from her sides as he looked his fill. Inside, she softened. Her nipples, already puckered, tightened even more.

Simon bent his head and licked her, his hair cold and smooth against the side of her breasts, his tongue sleek and hot. She shuddered. So did he. He bent to taste her again, drawing her fully into his mouth, licking and suckling until her head spun and her knees buckled. He caught her and carried her two short steps to the narrow padded bench. Wrapping his hard, warm arms around her waist, he stripped her of her panties.

His face was hard, piercing as a laser in its focus, incandescent with desire. Abashed by his intensity, she pressed her thighs together.

But he knelt before her on the puddled deck, opened her with his fingers and put his mouth on her. Pleasure speared through her, jagged, dark. She struggled to keep her feet, swaying toward the demand of his clever, insistent mouth, arching away, held helplessly in place by his hands and the shock of pleasure. He teased, tasted, devoured as her emotions rocked and tension swirled and gathered in her body.

She grabbed a handful of his hair and tugged. Now.

He rose to his feet and swept her off hers. She heard the almost audible click as his brain turned on, as he gauged the hardness of the deck and compared the narrowness of the bench with the distance to the cabin door.

She didn't want him to think. She wasn't drowning in this sea of feeling and sensation alone. She wanted him wild and naked and soon. *Now.* Twisting in his arms, she overbalanced and fell with him onto the padded seat. She straddled him. Kissed him. And felt the storm that gathered inside her jolt through him like lightning.

"Laura." Just her name, with a tiny undercurrent of laughter.

She fumbled with the elastic of his boxers, frustrated by the clinging cloth and their tight quarters. "What?"

Panting with triumph, dry-mouthed with desire, she freed him, hot and hard and hers. She closed her hand on him.

He groaned. "Condom."

Reality crashed on Laura like a wave. She knew better. She really did. And here she was about to repeat her mistakes like some moron.

She bit her lip and started to slither off his lap.

His hands clamped on her thighs. "Don't move. Just let me…" Simon leaned forward, reaching one arm to the floor, holding her to him with the other.

She clung to his smooth shoulders as he fished his pants from the deck and dug in the pocket for his wallet. He had a condom.

Hallelujah. She snatched the packet from him and ripped it open.

His hand trapped hers. "You don't mind?"

She didn't pretend to misunderstand. "That you carry a condom around in your wallet?"

Simon nodded, his breathing harsh. His body beneath hers was rock solid with tension. But his eyes were raw and naked with need. Her heart stumbled.

"How long has it been in there?"

"I bought them Friday. I thought with the party Saturday… There was a chance." He shrugged, his gaze level on hers. "Not very romantic."

If she felt a pang, she would have died rather than admit it.

"I told you I don't need romance." She smiled crookedly. "Anyway, right now I'd rather have this condom than a dozen red roses."

To prove it, she took his face between her hands and kissed him, raising herself on her knees so he could get the condom on. She caught her breath at the tickle of his rough chest against her breasts, the brush of his knuckles against her belly. Now. He was at her body's entrance, blunt and hot and seeking.

Slowly, slowly, she lowered herself, gasping as he stretched her, filled her, completed her. Their eyes locked. His were dark as rain clouds, swirling with emotion, shot through with need. He pushed himself up, inside her, deepening their connection, making her quake. She bit her lip to keep from crying out and lifted herself to do it again, the slick downward slide, the aching upward withdrawal. Now. Again.

Her thighs trembled on either side of his. His hands gripped her buttocks, bruising, commanding. She was fluid, flowing, everything inside her soft and lax except for the terrible, tightening spiral of desire. Sweat coated their bodies. Gleamed on his face. His breathing was ragged. Her blood drummed in her ears. She was blinded and burned by the sun pouring over her, by Simon moving under her and in her.

She tried to take, to hold, to possess, and could only receive. Absorb. Sensation rolled through her, too powerful to control, too big to contain. He drove up into her as far, as hard, as deep as he could go, and the tempest broke over them both. Battered, blinded, spun, she clung to him and cried out. He groaned and fell with her, shuddering, into the heart of the storm.

* * *

"I can't feel my legs," Simon said much later.

The observation didn't bother him as much as it should have. Laura lay limply over his spent body, her head on his shoulder, her breath warm against his neck. He had a cramp in his left calf and, he suspected, canvas burn on his butt from the padded seat.

He was completely relaxed. Wrecked. Satisfied.

Laura stirred, her damp flesh separating reluctantly from his. "I'll get off."

"No." His hands clamped on her tight, sexy rear. "You're fine where you are."

She was perfect where she was. She was perfect. If he had his way, he would stay with her like this forever.

She lifted her head. "I'm too heavy."

He studied the awareness returning to her dark, dazed eyes and flushed face. She was already retreating. Regrouping. He couldn't allow that. "You're impugning my manhood, Detective."

She sniffed. "Your manhood is in fine shape. Along with the rest of you. Now let me up."

"I can't."

"Why not?"

Inspired, he said, "We need to do it again."

"What?"

"It's the scientific method," he explained. "You formulate a theory. For example, 'Making love with Laura will be the best experience of my life.'"

She squirmed. "Oh, please."

If she wasn't ready to hear that he loved making love with her, she sure as hell wouldn't welcome the other words that weighted his tongue and crowded his heart. But he persisted, hoping she would see through his teasing to the desperate hope beneath.

"Do you want to learn about the scientific method or not?"

"Fine." She rubbed her cheek against his naked chest. Could she hear how his heart beat for her? "Teach me about the scientific method."

He tightened his arms around her. "Once you formulate your theory, you conduct an experiment that either proves or disproves the hypothesis."

"Huh. So, I'm an experiment now?"

"A highly successful one," he assured her. "But even after the desired results are obtained, a dedicated scientist will conduct subsequent experimentation to validate the truth of his hypothesis."

She cocked her head. "'Subsequent experimentation'?"

"Repeated subsequent experimentation," he said, straight-faced.

She held his gaze for a long, significant moment. Her smile broke slowly, beautiful as the dawn easing over the horizon. "That is the lamest excuse to have sex that I've heard in my life."

But she sighed and snuggled back against his shoulder.

He stroked her back, grateful to have this much of her. Wishing for more. "It's not lame. It's science."

It wasn't sex, either. It was making love.

Because if he evaluated all the data, if he considered all the evidence, this wasn't about chemistry anymore or respect or even "feelings."

He was falling in love with her.

A gull cried and wheeled over the lake. Water lapped against the side of the boat. Deep below deck, a motor switched on.

He should tell her, he thought. Hadn't they promised each other honesty? He could tell her now, while she was naked and boneless and receptive on top of him.

But he didn't want to destroy the peaceful aftermath of their loving. In his whole life, no woman had said those words to him, *I love you.* No one had wanted to hear them from him.

He'd never imagined saying them for the first time with his boxers pushed down around his thighs and chafe marks on his butt.

It wasn't…romantic, Simon decided, burying his own fears beneath excuses. Laura deserved romance. Wine. Moonlight. Flowers. Some damn thing.

And thought of her saying, *Right now I'd rather have this condom than a dozen red roses.*

His body stirred.

She stiffened. "What's that?"

"That" thickened and rose against her, eager for subsequent experimentation.

Simon laughed ruefully. "'That' is—"

"Smoke," she said, pushing up.

"What?"

"I smell smoke." She scrambled off his lap, snatching her T-shirt from the deck. "Where's your extinguisher? The boat's on fire."

Chapter 14

Fire.

Simon froze, his blood cold, his thoughts crystallizing. He yanked up his shorts. Oily curls of black smoke already seeped around the edges of the hatch to the engine compartment.

Laura clutched his arm. "Get out. Get off. We're going to blow up."

"The fuel's diesel, not gas. Grab the extinguisher from the galley," Simon ordered. That would take her forward, away from the fire and smoke, long enough for him to contain the fire. Assuming it had just started—*big assumption*—he had about two minutes to take it out. After that it would be too late.

Laura's eyes widened. She turned and dashed barefoot toward the cabin. Which would have been great, except under the circumstances he'd have to be stupid to feel relieved.

The air was growing hazy and hard to breathe. He needed to radio for help before the battery cables burned through.

Snatching the extinguisher from the bridge, Simon scrambled back to the engine compartment and pressed his palm to the hatch, feeling for heat from the fire below. His eyes burned. Yanking the safety pin at the top of the bright red cylinder, he took a deep breath and lifted the hinged cover.

Smoke billowed upward, searing, choking. He couldn't see a damn thing. Squeezing the discharge lever, he jammed the nozzle down and around, aiming for the engines eight feet away in the back of the boat. Foam shot out, coating the tangle of hoses and wires just below deck, cutting through the smoke. The cylinder hissed as it emptied.

He heard Laura burst through the cabin door behind him. She was coughing. He couldn't breathe. The smoke, oily, heavy, black, rolled over the deck. He knelt in the middle of it, squinting past the fumes and foam toward the orange-red glow of the fire, raking the base of the flames with the extinguisher. It sputtered and kicked.

Hell. He needed to put this fire out now. He needed...

The second cylinder clanked beside him. God bless Laura. Jerking the spent nozzle from the hatch, Simon reached for the new extinguisher. Laura had already pulled the pin.

He aimed. Squeezed. Sprayed. Choking gusts of chemical foam whooshed out. He didn't dare look away. His eyes ran. His nose, throat, chest burned. Sweeping the nozzle side to side, he blanketed the engine compartment.

The last orange flare subsided. Simon shot it again to be on the safe side—take that, you son of a bitch—and backed cautiously out of the open hatch. He retched, his eyes streaming.

Laura's bare feet wavered at the edge of his vision. "Is it out?"

He nodded, unable to speak, his throat aching and his heart raw with relief. She was safe.

"Here." She crouched beside him, pressing a wet towel from the galley into his hands.

He wiped his face gratefully. Sucked in his breath. And coughed so hard he almost threw up. The acrid stench of chemicals and smoke hung heavily over the deck.

"Come on." Laura tugged on his shoulder, her small hands impatient. "You need more air."

Simon staggered to his feet and stumbled forward with her. Soot blackened the canvas seat where they'd made love. He could have lost her. Even with the fire gone, the fear smoldered inside him.

Laura pushed him down on it and stood over him wearing nothing but a wet, grimy T-shirt and a scowl. "Are you all right?"

Her concern stroked his ego one way; ruffled it another. He liked her concern. He didn't want her pity. "Fine," he rasped.

"Yeah, I can hear how fine you are." She handed him a bottle of water. "Drink."

While he gulped gratefully, she padded across the wet, filthy deck and crouched by the hatch. Simon paused with the bottle of water to his lips. Her T-shirt rode high on her hips. She was naked beneath it. But her attitude was all business.

"The bilge is full," she called. "Must be a fuel leak."

He cleared his throat. "Or we're taking on water. I'll radio for help."

"Your radio's out. Fire must have gotten the wiring," she said absently, leaning over farther.

Simon sucked in his breath and coughed. Sweet God in heaven.

"I'll swim," he croaked when he could speak. "To the island. Use the phone at the house."

Laura nodded. "Yeah, you could do that. That would be really macho. Or if you'd rather not hike over rocks with no shoes and wet clothes, I could call on my police radio."

He laughed, chagrined. "That would save time."

"I thought so."

"Of course, we'd have to put on pants before they got here."

She shot him a grin, scooping her underwear from the deck. "Every plan has drawbacks."

He watched her step into her panties and draw them up her long legs and the curve of her butt. She was so beautiful and tough. Smart and funny. Just looking at her created a hollow in the center of his chest.

She rubbed the bridge of her nose, streaking her face with grime so that she resembled a very sexy commando. "Any idea how the fire started?"

Simon pulled himself together. No romance, he reminded himself. She didn't want compliments. She wanted theories. The lovemaking that had rocked his world, blown his mind and shaken his heart had already taken a back seat in her mind to the investigation.

If he hadn't laid all that respect stuff on her, he'd be a little put out.

Hell, Simon admitted, he was put out anyway.

He struggled to regain his customary detachment. "You said the bilge was full?"

She nodded and pulled off her T-shirt so she could put her bra on.

Simon stared, dry-mouthed. Think logically, he ordered himself. He was no use to her as this mass of sensation, this mess of emotion, this walking gland.

"If there was, ah, enough fuel in the hull, then any spark could have started a fire."

Laura fastened her bra and jerked her T-shirt back over her head. "But the engines were off."

The engines were off. But…

He remembered those moments right after she'd climaxed in his arms, when his world spun lazily with her at its center.

A gull cried and wheeled over the lake. Water lapped against the side of the boat. Deep below deck, a motor switched on.

A motor, Simon thought. The pump.

"The bilge pump has an automatic switch that senses the height of the water—or in this case, the water-and-fuel mixture. I heard it come on. If there was a loose connection in one of the wires, it could create the spark that caused your fire."

Laura's eyes widened. "Then it could have happened anytime. You could have caught fire on your way across the lake this morning."

"Or last night in the dark with guests on board."

Laura's eyes narrowed. "You had guests on this boat?"

"We used the cruiser to ferry people back to their cars. After…"

After her father's body struck the propeller of the rental boat and put it out of commission. He stood and reached for his pants.

"You're telling me all the suspects who came to the party last night had access to this boat," Laura said.

"Most of them." He stopped in the act of zipping his fly. *Suspects?* "Are you saying someone set the fire deliberately?"

"Why not?"

Why not?

Simon forced his hands to move, his brain to function. "Because no one had an opportunity. There must have been fifteen to twenty people on board at a time. Someone would have seen."

"It was dark. It was cold. What do you bet most of them stayed below? Anyone with a knife could slip out, lift the hatch and slice a fuel line in seconds."

"And risk blowing or burning themselves up?"

"It wasn't much of a risk," Laura argued. "You said the spark was caused by a bad connection in the bilge pump. It would take time for enough fuel to leak to turn the pump on. More than enough time for whoever cut the line to make the trip safely."

Simon frowned. He'd offered himself as bait last night. Were the rats really biting so soon? Or was Laura jumping at shadows in the corner? "Even if someone did cut the fuel line, he couldn't count on that faulty connection starting a fire. Or me being on the boat."

"What if he caused the spark? Loosened some wires or something."

"There wasn't time. There are too many wires down there to identify and isolate the right one."

Her chin stuck out. "Then maybe it was an impulse thing. A crime of opportunity."

"And maybe it wasn't a crime. Maybe it was an accident."

Laura grabbed the towel he'd used a moment ago to wipe his face. "Are you done with this?"

He eyed her warily. "Yes."

She marched back to the open hatch and dropped to her knees. Holding the towel, she lowered her arm below the fiberglass deck and wiped…something. She folded the towel to a clean section, reached and wiped again.

Simon's curiosity got the better of him. He strolled over to look over her shoulder.

"There." Laura sat back and pointed. The black rubber fuel lines, positioned for easy servicing of the filters, were only ten inches below the hatch opening. The distance from the fire had saved them from melting.

Simon squatted to take a closer look. His thigh brushed Laura's shoulder. The nearest fuel line was smeared in foam and soft with heat. But he could still detect the break in the hose, its edges sharp and deadly as a wound.

"That's a cut," Laura said tightly. "The fuel leak wasn't an accident. Somebody is trying kill you."

She'd screwed up, Laura acknowledged later that night as she leaned over the balcony of Simon's house. He had behaved like a hero, taking action, taking charge, saving her life when she was supposed to protect his. While she was still dazed by sex and dazzled by love, Simon had put out the fire in time to preserve both their lives and the evidence.

She couldn't afford another mistake. From now on, she would play smart. Play safe. Play cool. At seventeen, when she'd let herself get distracted by sex and swept away by her hormones, it had cost her her relationships with her father and her brother. This time it could cost her even more.

Because this time, she thought, listening to the rise and fall of Simon's voice from the dining room where he still sat with Dylan, this time she had so much more to lose.

And so she had endured the sly looks and teasing remarks of the rescue team when they'd arrived to salvage the boat and process the scene. She had made her report to the chief, painstakingly laying out the evidence in the face of his carefully noncommittal expression and in spite of her own discomfort at intruding—again—on his weekend.

Denko hadn't told her to stay away from Simon. But he had ordered her to stay out of trouble. There was a question in the police chief's eyes when he looked at her now, a reserve in his manner when he spoke to Simon. Laura couldn't tell if Denko suspected her of a breach of professional decorum or a failure of personal judgment, but his appraisal stung.

Maybe her judgment did suck. She could be mistaking sex for love. That would be female. Foolish. Like her. She had known Simon for less than two weeks. Maybe she was letting loss and loneliness and incredible sex blind her not only to what she had to do but to what she really felt.

But she didn't think so.

She hadn't just fallen for a hunky Mensa millionaire. Okay, the disciplined body and amazing mind were a definite plus. But she liked his integrity, his perception, his calm competence and cool humor. She admired the way he took care of others—stepmothers, siblings, employees—who only wanted to take from him.

No way was she joining their ranks.

She'd come back to the island with Simon tonight because he wasn't safe alone. But her focus had to be on this case. Her self-respect depended on it.

And so could his life.

"I want you to leave with Julie tomorrow," Simon told Dylan quietly.

His brother looked up from his cheesecake, his handsome face flushed. Wounded. "Sure. Whatever. I figured this family togetherness thing couldn't last."

The sneer was expected. The hurt was not.

"I've enjoyed having you here," Simon said, surprised to realize it was at least partly true.

Dylan tossed down his napkin. "Which explains why you can't wait to get rid of us. Or is it just that we're cramping your style with lovely Laura? Sorry," he mumbled in response to Simon's look. "You don't need a reason to kick us out."

But he did, Simon discovered.

"The accident this afternoon…" He hesitated. "I think it's

better for Julie, *safer* for Julie, if she goes back to school to-morrow. And I think it's better for you to stay at the condo for a while."

"Well, hell." Dylan stared at him, his golden movie star face slack. "You talk to Jules about this?"

Simon returned the look coolly. "No." He didn't want his sister to worry.

"Does this have anything to do with the break-in to your lab a week or so ago?"

Simon didn't answer.

Dylan swore again. "Who would want to go after you?"

Simon moved his knife a fraction of an inch to one side. "You might as well ask who benefits from my death."

"I do." Dylan drew a shuddering breath. "Julie and I do. My God, Simon—"

"I don't think Julie cut the fuel line on the boat last night," Simon interrupted him.

"Hell, no." Dylan looked directly at Simon, his eyes dark in his white face. "Do you think I did?"

There it was. The million-dollar question, Simon thought, his head and his heart both pounding. Could he trust Dylan? Could he trust his own judgment? Did he believe his own brother could hate him enough, or at least be indifferent enough, to want him dead?

"No," Simon said.

"Well, that's something." Dylan pushed his dessert away. "I wouldn't anyway, you know. Even if we weren't…" He stumbled, as obviously uncomfortable expressing emotion as Simon.

"Brothers," Simon supplied.

Dylan grinned. "Right. Even if we weren't brothers, it would be stupid. Like killing the goose that laid the golden eggs."

"Cultured gemstones," Simon said.

"Yeah. Now, if I was part of some big ruby cartel, it might make more sense."

"Why?"

"Well, an influx of low-cost, high quality stones on the market is definitely going to drive prices and profits down, at least in the short term. I'd take you out before you took my business away."

"Thanks," Simon said dryly. "That's very reassuring."

"Forewarned is forearmed. Anyway, you've got Laura around now to protect you."

"That is not why I want Laura around," Simon said, an edge to his voice.

Dylan raised both hands. "Hey, kidding. I know that. It's obvious from the way you look at the girl that you're crazy about her."

Was it? Simon brooded.

Then why hadn't she noticed?

Laura knew the exact instant Simon stepped out on the balcony. Her pulse quickened. Without turning her head, she said, "You were talking to your brother a long time."

The door scraped closed behind him.

"We had things to discuss," Simon said.

He leaned his elbows on the rail beside her, staring out at the darkening lake. His hard arm barely brushed hers. His scent—expensive soap, clean cotton, warm, relaxed male—drifted to her, seeping into her senses and soul. She could have stood like this with him forever, breathing him in, inhaling peace.

Think about the case, she ordered herself. Concentrate on your job. Or he might end up dead. There was a mistake she wouldn't recover from.

"I followed up on Dylan's alibi for last Wednesday night," she said abruptly. "It checks out."

Simon didn't move, but his very stillness told her he was suddenly a lot less relaxed. "You investigated my brother?"

"Yeah. Him and Quinn. Because of the passcard thing." She shrugged. "Of course, that was before E.C.I.P. sent us the computer log. But I thought it might be useful to know if he was lying about his whereabouts or activities that night."

"Is that what you and Denko were talking about this afternoon?"

"No, I talked to him about the cut in your fuel line."

"And?"

She chose her words with care. "And he agreed it looks suspicious."

"What else?"

Her throat was tight. "Nothing important."

"What else, Laura?"

Oh, God. She was vulnerable enough already. No way was she spilling her fears about the chief's shouted subtext, the restrained disapproval behind his clipped words, the I'm-disappointed-in-you-Baker look in his eyes.

But Simon was waiting for a response. Pressing her with his silence like an experienced interrogator.

She dug for another truth to give him, equally hurtful but less revealing. "Denko's concerned I can't be objective here."

"Because of your relationship with me," Simon said.

What relationship? Laura wanted to ask. They didn't have a relationship. They had a fake involvement to protect him until he got his full memory back, and they had sex.

Unless, please, God, he wanted more.

But he hadn't said anything about wanting more.

And she couldn't ask. Because if she did, and he didn't, it

would make things unbearably awkward between them. He might even ask her, gently and politely, to go.

And then who would protect him?

"Actually, it's because of my father," Laura said.

Simon straightened from the rail. "What about him?"

"Well, he's dead," Laura said. "He can't be a threat to you. So if I can prove you're still in danger, that would obviously help clear his name."

"Of course I'm still in danger. Somebody cut the damn hose."

"The chief's investigating that."

Simon raised his eyebrows. "And what am I supposed to do while he investigates? Stand out on Michigan Avenue and hope somebody takes a shot at me?"

The blood drained out of her head. She saw again his naked back bent over the hatch and the smoke billowing around him and felt dizzy.

"No," Laura said fiercely. "Denko made it very clear you're not to put yourself at risk."

"Until I know who's behind this, I don't know what's risky or not," Simon pointed out.

Neither did she.

Her failure so far to make progress on the case shook her confidence and stiffened her resolve. She was desperately afraid of letting Simon down, of disappointing him. If she couldn't do her job, what good was she?

But later that night when Simon came to her room, she did not turn him away. She opened her door and locked it behind him. Opened her robe and let it fall to the floor. Here, now, she could be what he needed. She could be who he wanted. She could show him, with urgent hands and eager lips, all the things she could not say, and he would not judge or reject her.

She pulled him with her onto the slippery cover of the wide guest bed, touching, squeezing, holding. Yet the more she tried to give him, the more he lavished on her in return. He threaded his fingers through her hair and cradled her head in his hands. He drank from her, sipping from her mouth and throat, savoring the crease of her elbow, the curve of her thigh. She shifted under him, restless as the wind that slipped through her window and stirred the tall curtains. He glided over her, sure and warm as the yellow lamplight beside their bed. He teased her and she trembled. Stroked her and she sighed. Moved on her and in her and she moaned.

"Shh," he whispered against her lips, his voice shaken with laughter and something else. "Shh."

"I want…" She tried again. "I should…"

"Let me." He kissed her eyelids. "Laura."

He linked their hands, palm to palm, fingers intertwined. Her breathing hitched. He trembled. She was wet, replenished, overflowing. She gave him everything she had, took everything he offered. And when the flood of sensation became too much, when feeling rose in her like a tide and swamped her heart, she held on to him for dear life and went down with him into the dark.

Simon woke reaching for Laura. She was gone.

He felt a surge of disappointment that had nothing to do with his rock hard state of readiness. Last night he'd made love to her as if he could push himself inside her often enough, embed himself within her deeply enough, imprint himself on her hard enough, to get under her skin. To make them one flesh.

Simon rolled to his side, smelling her on the sheets and the pillow, and heard the shower running. It took a minute, well, several seconds, for his brain to process the sound. Laura hadn't left. She was in the bathroom.

He could join her. Of course, first he'd have to go to his room for more condoms. Even though it was early—really early, the sky was still gray—he didn't relish the idea of running into his bright-eyed little sister as he tiptoed down the hall. But he thought about it. He fantasized about coming up behind Laura in the tiled stall, water pounding, steam rising, her body slick with soap and desire.

The water shut off. Okay. He could work with that, too. He pictured her coming out of the bathroom wearing nothing but a towel and a smile. No, it was his fantasy, skip the towel. She'd come out of the bathroom naked, her eyes softly glowing, and she'd reach for him and say...

"I don't know what time I'll be back. E.C.I.P. is sending someone over this afternoon so Quinn can go grocery shopping."

Simon opened his eyes. Laura was there. Standing by the bed, her smooth, tight body buttoned away in her uniform, her silky long hair twisted into a neat French braid.

He sat up against the crumpled pillows, pulling the sheet to cover his very obvious erection, feeling stupid, naked and at a disadvantage. "Where are you going?"

Her gaze stayed firmly on his face. Either she had excellent self-control or she didn't much care how she affected him. "It's Monday. I'm going to work."

He was dumbfounded. She didn't need a day taking care of traffic snarls, drunken fishermen and testy tourists. She needed to be taken care of herself. "Don't you get time off? Compassionate leave or something?"

"I'll request time off for the funeral, certainly," she said tightly. "But my shift ends at two o'clock. Plenty of time to make arrangements then."

He felt her slipping away where he couldn't reach her, couldn't help her, couldn't make her laugh or see her smile. "I'm not talking about funeral arrangements. I'm talking about giving yourself some personal time. Time to grieve. Don't you want to be with your brother today?"

She nodded. "I'm seeing him this afternoon."

She wasn't saying anything wrong. She wasn't doing anything wrong. Maybe that was the problem. Maybe he needed her to snap or cry or get sarcastic so he felt like he was dealing with Laura the warm, real, vulnerable human being instead of the Stepford Cop Girlfriend.

Patience and application, he reminded himself. Intimacy was a new experiment. Obviously there were some bugs to work out.

"Give me a minute and I'll go with you," he said.

"You should stay here. It's safer."

"Safer than the police station?" he asked dryly.

A flush dusted her cheekbones. "I won't be at the station all morning."

No, of course not. She had work. So did he.

"Afterward, then," he suggested. "We can get something to eat." He'd learned he could usually get around her with food.

But she shook her head. "I won't have time for that."

He heard, *I don't have time for you.* The refrain of his childhood.

But he wasn't a child anymore. And whether she knew it or not, whether she liked it or not, Laura needed him. Her father was dead. She was at odds with her boss. She had issues with her brother. He was it. Which suited him fine.

"All right," he said evenly. "We won't do lunch. I'll pick you up and take you to your brother's."

"You can't."

The hell he couldn't. He refused to let her shut him out. Close them down. "It'll be fine. I'll be fine. I can take care of myself."

"You don't get it," she snapped. "I can't afford another mistake."

Despite his awareness that this was the wrong time to push her, he was stung. "I wouldn't call our being together a mistake," he said carefully.

Come on, he thought. Give me something to work with here. Something to trust in. He felt like he was ten years old and waiting with the other boys at the start of summer vacation for his father to come, even though he knew damn well the only thing he'd see from home was a plane ticket to camp.

"Not a mistake," Laura amended. "A distraction."

He wasn't sure that was any better. But… "Maybe you need a distraction right now," he said.

"No, I don't. I have to set priorities. I don't need anything that's going to put you in danger or jeopardize my career."

I don't need you.

She didn't actually say the words. She didn't have to. It didn't take a genius to figure out that all she wanted from him right now was a graceful exit.

So he gave her one.

"Fine," Simon said. He didn't need her, either. "Don't let me stop you."

Her clear brown eyes clouded. "Will you be okay on your own?"

He was always on his own. Which was pathetic if he thought about it, but not nearly as pathetic as if he came right out and said it.

"Quinn's here," he said coolly. "And the guard's coming, right? Go do what you have to do."

Laura's lips parted. For a second Simon let himself hope

she was going to do something. Say something. Throw the dog a bone.

She took a deep breath and nodded and walked out of the room.

Chapter 15

Two o'clock. End of shift. Laura waited until the briefing room emptied to catch Denko in his office. She needed to prove to him and to herself that she was capable of putting personal feelings aside to get the job done.

She squared her shoulders. She was glad to be back in uniform, back in the station, on solid footing again. At least here she knew the rules. She didn't know the rules with Simon. Or even her own role. She was supposed to be taking care of him, wasn't she? Surely he would admit that saving his life was more important than salving his feelings? Which was why this morning it had been so important, so very important, so absolutely critical, that she leave his bed, turn down his lunch invitation and refuse his offer to come with her to visit her brother this afternoon.

So why didn't she feel better about it?

Denko's door was open. He looked up the instant before she knocked. "Laura. How are you doing?"

"Fine, Chief." Any other answer was unacceptable. Unthinkable. "Got a minute?"

"Actually, I wanted to talk to you before you went home. Close the door. Sit down."

She perched on the edge of her seat. "The autopsy was today."

"That's why I wanted to speak with you."

Oh, God. Her lungs crowded her throat. She swallowed. "Is… Has a formal identification of the body been made?"

"Yes. I'm sorry."

"Is it…"

"Your father." He nodded, his eyes compassionate. "Can I get you something? A glass of water?"

All she wanted was Simon, his arms around her, his calm, cool voice. "No, sir. I'm fine. Did the M.E. establish cause of death?"

"Drowning," Denko answered briefly.

Images of her father's mangled corpse flashed on her brain. She had to ask. She had to know, not only for her own sake, but for Simon's. "Just drowning?"

"The victim—your father was alive when he entered the water." Denko paused, as if debating with himself how much to tell her. "Certain wounds were undoubtedly inflicted post-mortem. However, there's also evidence to suggest that he sustained head trauma consistent with either a fall or a blow."

Laura squeezed her eyes shut. But that only made it easier to view the grisly mental slide show, to imagine her father sliding unconscious into the dark water.

A fall *or* a blow?

She opened her eyes. "So which was it?"

Another hesitation. "The M.E. can't say. Dan believes your father slipped and fell."

"And what do you think?"

"I think you need to trust your colleagues and turn your efforts to taking care of yourself and your family."

"My mother's dead," Laura blurted.

"But you have a brother," Denko said. "Older or younger?"

"Younger. Paul. I'm seeing him this afternoon."

Denko nodded. "Have you discussed with him where you'd like the body released?"

She wanted Simon and his PDA.

"Not yet," she said. "Can I get back to you on that?"

"Of course. There may be some personal effects you'll want, as well."

Laura shuddered. "I don't think so."

"His wedding ring, perhaps," Denko suggested gently. "A pocketknife. Keys."

Keys.

Laura straightened. "Was the master passcard recovered with his body?"

Denko's jaw tightened. "There was a card."

Laura's last hope—that somebody had stolen Pete Swirsky's passcard to gain admittance to the lab that night—died.

But she persisted. "Are you sure it's his card?"

"Other than that it has his name on it and was found with his body?" Denko asked dryly.

"It could be a duplicate," she suggested.

Denko's gaze sharpened. "Do you have any reason to believe that?"

Laura flushed. Reason? No. She was being completely unreasonable. But something deeper than reason drove her. Desperation. Instinct. Her gut.

"Doesn't each passcard have a traceable code? I just thought if you tested it…"

"I'll pass your suggestion on to Detective Palmer," Denko said.

Shut up, Baker. Quit while you're ahead. While you still have a job.

But the longer the investigation dragged, the longer Simon was in danger.

"I could take it to E.C.I.P. for testing this afternoon," she offered.

"No, you can't."

"It's no trouble. I'm going to Chicago to see my brother anyway."

"It's inappropriate. The victim's daughter cannot be part of the chain of custody. Any evidence in your possession could be challenged in court."

With each new development, she felt herself diminishing, her hard won identity disappearing.

"I'm not just the victim's daughter. I'm a detective in this department."

"I'm not questioning your credentials, Detective. Don't make me question your judgment. This is a very stressful time for you."

"I need to do something." The words burst from her like shrapnel.

"You can't do anything without jeopardizing the case. If not during the investigation, then in court. What you need is time to regain your perspective and deal with your personal business."

She was shaken. "You have no idea what I need."

"I think I do," Denko said. "Consider yourself on paid personal leave effective immediately."

Laura sat in her car with the engine running and the windows rolled, like a getaway driver or a suicide.

Paid personal leave.

Denko might as well have locked her in a holding cell. How was she supposed to function now? What was she supposed to do? She didn't want time to deal with her personal business. She didn't want to deal with anything personal. She was better at handling concrete evidence, even actual threats, than fears and feelings. She'd concentrated on the case because she was terrified of making a mistake on an emotional level.

And that may have been her biggest mistake of all.

Despite the blast from the car's air conditioner, her face, her throat, her whole body burned. Denko was right. She wasn't helping on this case. She couldn't. A few months as a rookie detective did not make her a better investigator than Denko himself. Or even Palmer.

The truth was, she found it easier to be a cop, to think, feel, react like a cop. She was more comfortable in the role of Simon's protector than Simon's lover. As long as she made herself responsible for his safety, she didn't have to accept responsibility for his feelings. Or her own. As long as she was necessary to the investigation, she didn't have to worry what other place she could possibly hold in his life.

I need to do something.

What you need is time to regain your perspective and deal with your personal business.

She reached for her cell phone. Fine. The first order of business was to talk to her brother. Maybe then she'd be ready to tackle the larger problem of Simon.

Yeah, and maybe pigs would fly.

When Paul didn't answer at home, she punched in the work number he'd given her yesterday. She drummed her fingers on the steering wheel as the line rang once. Twice.

"Executive, Corporate and Industrial Protection," the operator announced flatly. "How may I direct your call?"

Shocked, Laura disconnected.

She'd made a mistake. Her heart beat wildly. She'd misdialed. She must have.

Her fingers trembled as she checked the number in her notebook and entered it again.

"Executive, Corporate and Industrial Protection," the same voice droned. "How may I direct your call?"

Oh, God. Okay.

Laura drew a deep breath. "Is Paul Swirsky there?"

The operator was going to say no. She had to say no. Because if she said yes, that would mean… Well, Laura wasn't certain what it meant, but she was sure it would be bad.

"One moment," the operator said, and then her brother's voice came on the line.

"Swirsky."

Oh, God, Laura thought. It was a plea. A prayer. *God, make my brother innocent. God, keep Simon safe. Please, God, don't let me mess this up.*

"Paul, it's Laura. I'm coming to see you, okay? We need to talk."

Simon slid the platinum crucibles back into the furnace. Dissolving aluminum oxide in a molten salt with the right amounts of chromium at just the right temperatures to form ruby crystals was exacting and painstaking work. It kept his mind and his hands occupied.

And if his heart occasionally demanded what the hell he was doing sulking in his lab instead of chasing Laura to Chicago, well, when had he ever listened to his heart?

In the lab, he was in control of the reactions that would produce the desired results. If A, then B. He understood the process.

Simon frowned and adjusted the temperature of the furnace. He couldn't control Laura's reactions. She wasn't logical. She wasn't predictable. Understanding her was a damn sight harder than mastering a chemical equation.

He watched the magma glowing and blazing within the pots and thought, *She isn't fake, either.*

The intercom on the wall hummed and popped. Quinn's voice said, "Mr. Ford? Dwayne Cooper's here from E.C.I.P. I'm going shopping now."

Recognition buzzed and bumbled at the back of Simon's brain like a fly against a window screen, not really a memory, not quite an identification. His mind playing hide-and-seek again. He brushed it away. "Thank you, Quinn."

"Do you need anything?"

Unfortunately the thing Simon wanted most Quinn couldn't pick up for him at the store.

"No, thanks," he said. "I'm fine."

Laura sat on a corner of the desk in her brother's cubicle feeling like Sibyl the multiple personality wacko. She was having enough trouble handling investigating cop, suspect's daughter and victim's pseudo girlfriend without adding you-can-tell-me-anything-I'm-your-big-sister to the mix. "So, have you talked with anybody from the police yet?"

Paul looked confused, but she wasn't sure if that was because of her question or her sister act. "Why would I talk to the police?"

"Because they're investigating Dad's disappearance." And a robbery. And attempted murder. She squashed a squiggle of guilt.

"Oh. No." Paul rubbed his face with his hands. He had their mother's thin face, their dad's big hands and a really bad haircut. "Jeez, I can't believe he's gone."

Laura swallowed the lump in her throat. "Me, either," she confessed. "Kind of like pushing against a door all your life and then it opens and you fall flat on your face."

Paul laughed and then sobered. "You always resented that he liked me better than you."

Her stomach cramped. "Let's not go there, okay? I'm glad you two got along."

Paul sulked. "I didn't say that. He wasn't exactly easy to get along with."

"Would you say he had enemies?" Laura asked carefully.

"Yeah, I guess he—" Paul's gaze narrowed. "Why? What's all this about?"

She was so not supposed to go there. She wasn't only off the case, she was temporarily off the force—on enforced leave, only a prayer and a step away from suspension. But what were her options? Go back to Denko? *Hey, Chief, about that investigation you ordered me to stay away from because of my personal involvement? Funny thing, but my brother works for the same security company as my old man.* Yeah, they'd bust a gut laughing over that one.

She was too inexperienced. Too emotionally involved. Too close.

Simon's voice came back to her, steadying, strengthening. *Maybe you're the only one close enough to see at all.*

She looked into her brother's suspicious eyes and told the truth. Part of it, anyway. "The police are investigating the possibility that dad's death wasn't an accident."

"Why?"

"I can't tell you. Some of it has to do with who had access to the Lumen Corp security system and when."

Paul frowned. "I already gave my boss that list like a week ago."

Her mouth dropped open. "*You* did?"

"Yeah. I'm chief assistant pencil pusher and badge boy around here."

Her heart beat quicker. "Can I see it? The list?"

Paul swiveled his chair around to his computer. "My boss would kill me if he knew I was doing this."

"Mine, too," Laura muttered.

"What?"

"Never mind." She looked over his shoulder, where neat columns of names and numbers appeared on the screen. "Tell me what I'm looking at."

"Huh? Well, the long number on the left is the access code. You can see the first four digits are the same—that's the Lumen Corp code—and then the rest identify the department and the individual card number. Each card is different. And next to that is the date the card was issued and the person it was issued to."

Laura scanned the columns, searching for omissions, deviations, discrepancies. Each card had a card holder. The passcard belonging to her father had been deactivated, but none were missing. "What's that?"

"Where?"

She pointed to the left hand column. "There's a break in the numerical sequence."

"Oh, that." For the first time Paul looked uneasy. "That's nothing."

"Why does the list skip a number like that?"

"It doesn't really matter now."

Her eyes narrowed. "Then you can tell me about it."

Paul rubbed his face with his hand again. "Okay. I guess it's too late to get in trouble about it."

"About what?"

"Dad misplaced his passcard a couple of weeks ago. The company docks you fifty bucks for a lost card, so I made him a replacement until the old one turned up." Paul shrugged. "I figured when he found the old card, I'd hang on to the new one and assign it to the next new hire. Only Lumen Corp hired another guard, so I had to enter another number into the system."

Laura's system jolted. Not that nice little prickle like static electricity that most cops recognized as a hunch, either, but a high wattage shock. *This is it.*

"You gave Dad an extra card."

"Yeah."

"He asked you to?"

"Yeah. Well, he agreed."

"So it was your idea?" That made more sense. She couldn't see their by-the-book father bending the rules, even to get out of a fifty-dollar fine.

"Kind of. Dwayne gave him the card."

"Who's Dwayne?"

"Just a guy. A friend. He was doing Dad a favor."

"What's his name again?"

"Dwayne. Dwayne Cooper."

"So he talked Dad into taking the card."

"I guess. He took it to him."

Her pulse jumped. Took it to him? Or stole it? But no, that didn't make sense either. The unauthorized copy wasn't used to access Simon's lab that night. Laura studied the columns as if the numbers were going to add up and tell her something. Anyway, Cooper's name was right there on the list. He had his own master passcard.

But that whine of excitement refused to die.

Unless Cooper took their father's card to pin the blame on him? Or…

"Cooper's card was issued after you made that copy for Dad," she observed.

Paul nodded. "He's filling Dad's slot at Lumen Corp."

The whine grew to a howl. "Was he working Saturday night?"

Paul tapped the keyboard and pulled up another screen. "Yeah, he was doing event security for some big shindig north of the city."

Simon's party. She thought of the cut fuel line, and her chest felt tight. "Where is he now?"

Paul shrugged. "At work, I guess."

"At the park? Or with Simon?"

"What do you mean?"

"Is Cooper assigned to personal security?"

"I can check." Another screen appeared. "Executive protection today. He's covering Simon Ford."

She was already punching Denko's number into her cell phone. "Tell your boss you're leaving early," she ordered Paul over her shoulder. "We're going to Eden."

The telephone rang and fell silent.

Simon raised his head from his notes, hoping to hear the intercom announce Laura Baker on line one. It didn't. He didn't expect it to.

Did he? The question bobbed up, ugly and unexpected as a body in the lake.

He was waiting for her to make the first move. She was the one who'd rejected him. And he'd reacted the way he always did, withdrawing to his lab like a sulky boy to his room, burying himself in his work, hoping she would…what? Come after him?

Well, yes.

Why do women always have to do all the work?

She was the one who set limits on their relationship, he thought, trying to hold on to his indignation. He'd told her he had feelings for her, hadn't he? Made love to her with everything that was in him. Offered her support through a difficult time. And when she'd brushed him off, he'd said… He'd said…

Simon frowned. He'd said, *Don't let me stop you. Go do what you have to do*.

He was a fathead. And a coward.

While Laura worried about his danger, he'd been protecting himself all along. He hadn't done one thing to put himself at emotional risk.

And when she'd bared herself in the sunlight and offered herself to him, he'd been so keen to have her naked and in his arms that he'd accepted her easy terms. *I'm available. You're interested. So what's the deal?*

He flipped shut his notebook and carried it to the safe. The deal was he wanted more, wanted her shoot-from-the-hip honesty and disarming warmth across his table in the morning and in his bed at night. He wanted her to add color to his sterile walls and solitary life.

He wanted her more than she needed him. And the realization shook his confidence and scorched his pride.

So what was he going to do about it?

He slipped the notebook in beside the other painstaking recreations of his recent work. And felt a shiver of body memory, like a shadow across the back of his neck. He almost flinched. Carefully, he closed the safe, locked it and turned.

A guard in a recognizable black uniform with a vaguely familiar face stood at the entrance to the lab.

And behind him was…

"Vince?" Simon frowned. "What are you doing here?"

"I know you're worried." Even through the distortion of Laura's cell phone, Jarek Denko's voice was reassuringly calm, inflexibly cool. "But we don't know yet that there's an immediate threat."

Laura shifted her phone to her other ear and changed lanes at eighty miles an hour. Her brother Paul grabbed the arm-rest. "We know I can't get through to the island by phone."

"Is the number in service?" Denko asked.

Damn it. "Yes," Laura admitted reluctantly.

"Then the line hasn't been cut," the chief said reasonably.

"But he hasn't picked up."

"The last time I checked, that wasn't a crime. Ford could be working."

"He could be dead," Laura snapped.

Or Simon could have decided not to talk to her ever again after her stilted, nightstick-up-the-butt exit this morning. But she wouldn't bet his life on it.

"You said there's a security guard there with him now?" Denko asked.

Laura's knuckles were white on the steering wheel. "A guard who may have had access to the lab the last time Simon was attacked."

She whipped around a truck on the right, missing what-ever Denko said next. Paul braced his feet against the floor-boards. They were still five miles outside Eden. "What?"

"I said, I'll send someone out there to take a look," the chief repeated patiently. "Make sure everything's all right."

Anxiety flared in Laura's chest. "If there is a situation, a police presence could trigger a crisis."

"Or prevent one," Denko said.

"You should send somebody who has another reason to be there," Laura said. "I could go."

Say yes, say yes, say yes, she urged silently, as if the phone could beam her message directly into his brain.

"No," Denko said. "Come in and we'll talk."

Oh, God, she wanted to do it his way. To give up responsibility and go back to playing by the rules.

"There isn't time to talk. We need to do something."

"I am not calling in a tactical operations unit because your boyfriend won't answer the phone," the chief said astringently.

Despair hollowed her chest. "If you'd just talk to my brother—"

"I want to talk to your brother. Bring him in, we'll assess the threat and take whatever action is necessary."

By then, Laura thought bleakly, it would be too late. Her hands clenched. Her heart clenched.

She ended the call and tried to reach Simon again, punching in the numbers one-handed as her little red GT shimmied around the off ramp. Ring, ring, ring. *Damn you, Simon, pick up.* No answer. They shot down Old Bay Road at fifteen miles an hour over the speed limit.

Simon wasn't her boyfriend, Laura thought, hanging grimly on to the wheel. She wasn't his girlfriend. She was a cop, and her chief had just given her a direct order to stay away from the island and come in. She was already in trouble. She couldn't afford to screw up again.

And none of that mattered a damn now.

Simon's life was on the line. She wouldn't walk away from him again. Her role as Simon's girlfriend was an act. But her feelings were real. She loved him.

Maybe Denko was right, she thought as she swerved to the curb in front of the police station. Maybe she was overreacting. But maybe she wasn't, and Simon was alone on the island with an armed guard who'd killed once and was prepared to kill again.

She jerked to a stop in front of a fire hydrant. "I need you to talk to my boss," she told Paul. "Ask for Chief Denko."

He swallowed. "Aren't you coming in with me?"

"No time."

"But what do you want me to tell him?"

"The truth." She leaned across him to open the passenger side door. "Everything. Go."

"Are you—"

She wasn't sure how much he'd picked up from her half of the phone conversation, but there was no time for explanations. "Yeah."

Paul met her gaze. For one moment he was her little brother again, looking at her with love and trust in his eyes. "Be careful," he said, and got out of the car.

Her heart was too full for speech. She peeled away from the curb, praying she wasn't already too late.

Chapter 16

Wrong question, Simon thought, his stomach knotting. He knew what Vince Macon was doing here. He just didn't have a clue why.

Vince smiled, his eyes hard, looking as if he'd strolled out of a shareholders' meeting, except he was wearing a golf shirt and khakis instead of a suit and tie. "You're a remarkably difficult man to discourage," he said.

Vince was behind this? All of this? The theft, the attack, the attempt on his life? But why?

"I could say the same about you," Simon said coolly. Could he reach the panic button on the intercom? But what good would that do? Quinn was shopping. And if the alarm rang at E.C.I.P., they would want to speak to their guard— the broad faced young man holding the gun.

The snub, black gun. The gun pointing at Simon. Simon

looked from its muzzle into the eyes of the guard and felt the slippery knot in his stomach get tighter.

Well, hell.

"Open the safe," Vince said.

Simon raised his eyebrows. "Once wasn't enough?"

"You don't think I'll actually answer that."

"I'm surprised, that's all. I thought you didn't like my cultured rubies."

"Fakes," Vince sneered.

"Then why take them?"

Vince pulled in his chin like a politician faced with scandal. "Because valueless as they are, they have the potential to drive down the value of the entire market."

Simon remembered what Dylan had said about the impact of the low-cost, perfect stones on the ruby market.

"So you're invested in gemstones, too?"

"I'm not discussing my portfolio with you, Simon. Open the safe."

"There are no stones in there."

"I don't want your stones," Vince said impatiently. His hard gaze flicked to the guard.

So Vince hadn't taken the rubies. But maybe his accomplice had. A slow rage rose in Simon's blood. He recognized the security guard now. This was the bastard who had put his hands on Laura. And murdered her father?

"Then what are you going to do with them?"

"They'll be disposed of. Slowly. I have to protect my investments. All my investments."

"Is that why Cooper here didn't kill me the first time?"

"You're worth much more to me alive," Vince said. "I thought it would be enough to take a few notebooks. Perhaps divert suspicion to your brother."

But he'd recreated his notes, Simon thought. And when

he'd supported Dylan and his plans to market the rubies at the party, that must have been the last straw.

"Your mistake," he said.

"My mistake was in not cutting my losses and moving on. I don't intend to repeat it." Vince nodded to Cooper.

Cooper grinned. A report echoed against the lab's ceiling.

Simon felt a slap on his arm. He stared down in disbelief at the ragged edges of his sleeve, the raw furrow through his flesh. He'd been shot. The son of a bitch had actually shot him, he thought with the part of his brain that hadn't closed down in shock. Blood welled, staining the shirt, dripping on the pristine floor. Pain followed. Simon hissed through his teeth.

"Open the safe," Vince repeated.

"Or what?" Simon said. His arm burned. "You'll shoot me?"

Cooper turned his head toward the tall windows overlooking the lake, his gun never wavering from Simon. "Somebody's coming."

Thank God.

"It's the girl."

Simon's relief evaporated. His heart hammered against his ribs. Laura? Not Laura.

"Maybe she'll go away," Vince said.

Not if it was Laura. She was too dogged to quit. Her determination was one of the things he loved about her. But now he wished she would turn tail and run.

"She's seen our boat," Cooper said. "She's coming up."

The knots in Simon's stomach assumed Gordian proportions.

Vince pursed his lips. "All right."

"You don't want to hurt a cop," Simon said. Kill a cop. Kill Laura. Sweat trickled down his back.

Cooper smirked. "I don't mind."

Son of a *bitch*.

Simon kept his gaze on Vince, his voice cool and persuasive. "Other cops get upset when it's one of their own. So do juries, if it comes to that."

"Not if there aren't any witnesses," Cooper said. "I'll take the door."

Terror stopped Simon's breath and almost froze his brain. The guard was going to shoot Laura from cover as she approached the house. She wouldn't have a chance.

"I could send her away," he said desperately. "Let me talk to her."

"You must think I'm stupid," Vince said. "Why would I let you do that?"

Simon's arm burned and throbbed, making it difficult to think. "Let me send her away, and I'll open the safe."

"What about…" Vince gestured to the bloody graze in Simon's arm.

"I'll wrap it. Or you can wrap it. Just let me send her away."

"I'm not coming near you," Vince said. "But if you can cover that up before she reaches the house, I'll let you talk to her."

Laura lifted her head. Gunshot. Up at the house. The sound smacked her hearing and rattled around inside her chest like a lead slug. *Simon.* Her heart died.

She launched herself at the path that led to the house, radioing for help as she ran under the cover of trees. *Too late, too late, too late…*

"Request backup on a shooting in progress on Angel Island, shooting in progress, Angel Island."

"Assistance en route," the dispatcher said breathlessly. "Stand by. Do you copy?"

No way in hell was she standing by.

"Negative. I'm going in."

The radio sputtered. She flipped it off, concentrating on her approach.

She didn't have a passcard, damn it. Being Simon's girl-friend, even his pretend girlfriend, ought to include having a key.

Sliding her gun from its holster, she surveyed the windows and doors. There was a chance no one was monitoring the security system inside. Anyway, marching to the front door after hearing a gunshot was a sure invitation to getting her head blown off.

The balcony was her best bet, she decided. But before she could slip into the shrubbery along the side, she caught a shadow wavering in the glass by the front door.

She tensed. The door opened.

Simon.

Her heart gave a great leap and lodged in her throat.

He looked pale. Preoccupied. Annoyed. "Laura? What are you doing here?"

"That's a hell of a welcome," she said, lowering her weapon. "Aren't you going to invite me in?"

He frowned. "I'm working."

Working? Outrage momentarily robbed her of breath. Well, he was wearing a lab coat. She'd never seen him in one before.

"I'll wait," she said.

He drew a sharp breath. He looked like hell.

Her cell phone bleeped. She ignored it. "Are you all right?"

"Why wouldn't I be?"

Something was wrong. She felt it like a spider on the back of her neck. She tightened her grip on her gun. "Where's the guard? Cooper?"

Simon raised one shoulder slightly, shrugging off her concern. "He went into town. With Quinn."

"You sent him away?" Hope and disbelief cracked her voice.

"I'm working," Simon said again, impatiently, like an advanced math teacher forced to explain a simple concept for the umpteenth time to a remedial student. He met her eyes. His were cold. "I don't like having people around me while I work."

Well. Laura fought the burning in her throat, the sudden chill in her bones. That was certainly clear.

If she had any pride, if she had any sense, she'd radio to cancel backup and then crawl away into a hole to contemplate her broken heart and the wreckage of her career.

She stuck out her chin. "What about me?"

"You said it yourself this morning," Simon said evenly. "You have your priorities. I have mine."

"You pompous ass," Laura said.

He winced. Recovered. He really did look bad. Ill, almost.

Laura scowled. She was here because she loved him, the clueless jerk. And she wasn't letting him send her away until she was sure he was safe.

"Let me in," she ordered. "I'm staying until Quinn gets back."

Simon blocked the door with his body. Sweat beaded his face. "Laura, no. I don't want—"

"Drop it," a new voice ordered from behind the door. "Or I'll kill you."

Laura's hand tightened on her gun. Too late. Vince Macon stepped in behind Simon, his own body protected by the open door, the .22 in his hand pressed to the back of Simon's skull. No way could she level her weapon in time.

Her cell phone shrilled again. Denko, calling to demand an assessment of the situation.

Vince jerked visibly. "What the hell is that?"

"My backup," she said boldly. "They're on the way."

She hoped.

"Really? My backup is behind this door waiting to blow a hole in you and your boyfriend," Vince said. "So put down your damn gun."

Crap. Okay. As long as she was alive, she had a chance. As long as Simon was alive, she had hope.

"Don't do it," Simon said.

Ignoring him, she lowered the Glock and laid it on the steps at her feet. She couldn't risk another mistake. She couldn't risk him.

As she straightened, the door yanked open. A big guard in the black E.C.I.P. uniform—Tweedledum. Cooper?—hustled out and scooped up her gun, sticking it in his belt. Vince kept his gun pressed to Simon's head.

The guard stripped the cuffs from Laura's waist and secured her arms behind her, jerking up once on her bound wrists. Pain knifed through her shoulder blades. She bit back a cry.

"All right," Vince said. "Downstairs."

"What do you want?" she asked as they were herded below.

"My notes," Simon said tersely. "My research."

"Aren't your ideas, like, patented? Protected?"

"He doesn't want to use my ideas. He wants to destroy them."

"Shut up," Cooper said.

And that's when Laura got it. If Macon really wanted to keep Simon's technology off the market, he needed to do more than destroy Simon's notes. Simon had already proved he could recreate his research. Macon needed to destroy him.

Terror clogged her throat. She glanced over her shoulder

at Simon to see if the same thought had occurred to him. His face was grim. Pale. Collected.

Her mind raced. The only way Simon could stay alive was if he didn't open the safe. As long as his research survived in note form, Macon couldn't kill him.

"Stop staring," Cooper said, and shoved her down the last three steps. With her arms bound, she couldn't catch herself. He laughed as she stumbled.

The phone trilled again.

"Can't you turn that damn thing off?" the guard snarled.

"Go ahead," Laura said.

That would get Denko here in a hurry. Though after her radio call, she hoped—prayed—the chief was already on his way.

Vince shot them an annoyed glance. "Leave it. Open the safe," he ordered Simon.

With horror, Laura registered red seeping on the arm of Simon's lab coat. He'd been shot. These rat bastards had shot him. She wanted them dead.

Simon tilted back his head and looked down his nose. "Sorry. You lost your chance when you didn't let Laura go."

"I took a chance," he corrected. "And now I'm going to take everything." He nodded to the guard, who turned his gun on Laura.

"Open the safe," Vince said. "Or Cooper, here, will shoot your girlfriend."

Simon stiffened.

"That would be a really bad idea," Laura said. "You're going to piss off a bunch of cops if you do."

"Why, when I tell them how devastated I was to witness your tragic fight with your boyfriend? Poor Ford. He was so overcome with remorse he turned his gun on himself."

"You've been watching too much TV," Laura said. "My boss will never buy that."

"You won't be around to know. Unless…" Vince looked meaningfully at Simon.

"Don't do it," Laura begged Simon. "He'll shoot me anyway."

Vince showed his teeth in a smile. "Yes, but where? And how often? Do you really want to hear her scream as Cooper shatters one kneecap after another? Or empties his gun into her gut? I've heard that's a very prolonged and painful way to die."

"Screw you," said Laura.

"That is, of course, another alternative, but I don't think we have time. Too bad."

Simon took a step forward.

Vince leveled his gun. "The safe."

"Don't do it," Laura said. "Don't give them what they want."

"I warned you I can be very clear in my instructions," Vince reminded him. "Do you want to hear me tell Cooper exactly what I want him to do?"

"You don't need to," Simon said, his voice harsh. "I'll open it."

"No," Laura cried.

Cooper hit her. She didn't see it coming, couldn't have prevented it anyway with her hands locked behind her. Just… Pow. Stars, pain, exploding in her jaw and neck as she flew several feet and crashed into a lab table. And then pain in her side and blood in her mouth.

She spat it at him.

He raised his arm again.

"Enough," Simon shouted. "I said I'd open the damn safe. Don't touch her."

"We've made our point, I think," Vince said.

Cooper wavered on the edge of violence. He wanted to hit her again, Laura realized. He enjoyed hitting her.

She wondered if she could taunt him into hitting her long enough to buy them more time. Time for Denko to come to their rescue. Time to save Simon's life.

But Simon had already crossed to the wall safe.

"Open it and back away," Vince said.

"There's an inner safe," Simon said, as he entered numbers on the keypad. "A kind of box. I have to take it out to open it."

"You didn't have anything like that before," Cooper said.

Simon spared a glance over his shoulder. "Precisely."

"All right," Vince said. "But slowly. I want to see your hands."

Laura straightened painfully. They all watched as Simon turned from the safe with a metal shoebox-looking thing in his hands. His sleeve was red. His face was white. Lines of strain bracketed his mouth. How much blood had he lost?

"Looks heavy," Cooper said. "What've you got in there?"

"Notebooks, mostly." Simon set it carefully on a table.

In the silence, Laura's phone started ringing again. Vince jerked. Cooper swore. Both men were sweating. Time was running out for all of them.

Simon shifted the box slightly. His eyes narrowed in concentration. He made an adjustment. Entered a code. The box hummed.

Vince frowned. "What are you—"

Cooper grunted and froze like a statue.

Simon's quiet, lecturing voice came back to Laura. *At the right frequency, the current stimulates the muscle fibers to a single sustained contraction. Tetanization. Temporary paralysis. Phasers on stun.*

Oh, my God.

Cooper was paralyzed. Really paralyzed.

Vince was not. And Vince still had his gun aimed at Simon.

"Cooper," Vince snapped without looking at his henchman.

Cooper didn't respond. Couldn't respond. His face was faintly pink.

"Cooper!" Vince turned his head. The gun wavered.

And Laura, seeing her chance, went in fast and hard.

Vince gaped, bringing the gun around as she sprang. Her boot slammed his crotch. The gun discharged by her ear—*flash! bang!*—close enough to feel the heat. Off balance, blinded, she fell, and heard a window shatter.

"Laura!" Simon yelled.

She scrambled, writhing on her side, desperate to throw herself onto the gun before Vince recovered and grabbed it. Moaning, he uncurled, stretching out his arm.

Simon stumbled over the other man's legs and stooped for the gun.

"Police!"

Laura registered the shouts, the thud of running feet. They came through the window and down the stairs. Suddenly the room was full of uniforms.

And every one of them had his weapon trained on Simon, holding the gun. He froze.

Laura screamed. "No!"

"Hold fire," Jarek Denko ordered, glass crunching beneath his feet. "Baker, are you all right?"

She struggled to sit. Her head and jaw throbbed. She could taste blood. "Yes, sir."

"He hit her," Simon said. "Jaw and side of the head. She fell into a table."

"They shot him," Laura said. "He needs transport to the hospital."

"Already on the way," Denko assured her. "You want me to take a look?" he asked Simon.

"I'm fine."

He wasn't fine, Laura thought worriedly. His sleeve was soaked with blood, his arm at an awkward angle.

Crouching, Simon looked around warily at the uniforms, all aiming at him. "Or I will be once someone takes this damn gun."

"Larsen," Denko said.

The officer lowered his shotgun and stepped up to relieve Simon of his weapon. The tension in the room eased.

Denko looked down at Vince Macon on the floor and then over at Dwayne Cooper. The guard still hadn't moved a muscle. His face was an alarming red.

"What the hell happened to him?" the chief asked.

Simon shuffled to the table, his back stiff, his steps dragging. "This is a prototype of a muscular tetanization device. I need to…" He adjusted the controls.

"A what?" Denko asked.

"Phasers on stun," Laura said absently. She was watching Simon. Compared to Cooper, who now glowed, the inventor's face was pasty white. She felt a thrill of anxiety. "You know, like *Star Trek?* Can somebody get these cuffs off?"

"Sure."

At Denko's nod, Rick Whelan came over and squatted by Laura. "Where are the keys?"

"On the boat. *Damn* it."

Cooper groaned and started to tremble.

So did Simon.

"Simon?"

Laura pushed herself to her feet. With her arms secured behind her, she could only watch helplessly as he slid to the floor.

Too late, too late, too late…

* * *

Simon floated, tethered to the outside world by the hard, flat mattress under his back and the tube running into his arm. Alone in his mind with the pain.

His brain was foggy. His mouth was dry. His arm hurt like hell. The air was sterile. Alien. Phones rang. Lights buzzed. By his head, a monitor blipped and hummed.

He'd always had a thing for machines. That didn't mean he wanted to wake up hooked up to one.

He shifted to get away from it, and his hand brushed something soft. Warm. Alive.

He opened his eyes. Laura.

She hunched in a chair by his bedside, her folded arms resting on his mattress, her bowed head resting on her arms, asleep. A great wave of love and gratitude took him by the throat. Her face turned toward him. Her lip was swollen and bleeding. Her jaw, what he could see between her arm and her hair, was puffy and discolored. He'd never seen anyone more beautiful in his life.

He stretched cautiously to touch her again, and she woke up.

For an instant they stared at one another. Her eyes were wide and dark. His pulse and respiration went so crazy he expected the machines on the wall to start bleeping or something.

Laura licked cracked lips. "You jerk. You scared me to death."

Simon smiled. He let himself touch her, running his fingers over her smooth hair, her poor, battered face. "You scared me, too. Are you all right?"

"Stiff," she admitted, rolling her shoulders. "Sore."

"That's what you get for sleeping in a chair." Don't read too much into it, he told himself. Don't scare her away. "How long have you been here?"

Her gaze slid away. "A while."

Now that he was more awake, he noticed things. The darkness outside the window. The collection of cups by her chair. "How long have I been here?"

"Since eight o'clock. Chief called Medevac for you," Laura said. "The gunshot wound's not that bad, but you had significant loss of blood."

He glanced at the bedside clock. It was just past two in the morning. "Have you been here the whole time?"

"Yeah." Her thin face flushed in the dim light. "I had to make up some story about how you'd want to see me when you woke up."

Hope hooked its claws in him, tenacious as pain.

"Laura." He waited until he had her full attention. "I do want to see you. There's no one in the world I'd rather wake up with."

Her throat moved as she swallowed. "Gee," she said gruffly. "That makes me feel all warm and fuzzy."

He couldn't tell if she was kidding or not. But he wasn't. He loved her. And it was time he told her so.

"There's something we need to discuss."

She nodded. "My father. I know."

Maybe whatever painkillers they'd slipped into his IV were making him stupid. "What about your father?"

"I talked to the chief. Both Macon and Cooper are in custody and talking, trying to pin as much of the blame as they can on each other. When Vince realized your laser 'by product' could threaten his gemstone investments, he hired Cooper to stop its development. Cooper wanted the job, so he didn't tell Vince he didn't have access to Lumen Corp. Instead, he stole my father's passcard and talked my brother into making Dad a new one on the Q.T. Dad probably never knew about the substitution."

"There was an extra guard that night," Simon said, the memories stirring like dark things underwater.

Laura looked at him sharply.

"I remember," he said. "I didn't think anything of it at the time, because he had on the same uniform. I'd opened the safe, and…"

"And he knocked you on the head and took your journal and the rubies."

"But he didn't count on your father," Simon said quietly.

"Dad apparently surprised him as he was getting into his boat. Cooper claims they struggled and Dad's death was an accident. Chief Denko thinks it's more likely Cooper saw the opportunity to pin the theft on somebody else. Everyone would assume the missing guard and the missing rubies were connected."

"Everyone did," Simon said. "Except you."

She shrugged. "I was lucky, spotting the passcard thing."

"No," Simon corrected gently. "You're good. Your father would have been proud of you."

She flushed.

"So, what happens now?" Simon asked, struggling to sit up.

She found the controls that raised his bed. "Palmer and Denko are putting together the case. It's going to be big for our little department. Macon's in jail. Cooper's under guard and under observation here at the hospital. The doctors aren't sure what's wrong with him. His vitals are fine, but he's got some weird skin condition, almost like—"

"Sunburn," Simon said.

"Yeah." Laura looked at him with surprise. "How did you know?"

"The electrical charge for the MTD is delivered along UV rays," Simon explained. "Concentrated in one area for too long, it can create a burn effect. Like sunburn."

"I'll tell the chief. He was pretty impressed with your Mr. Wizard thing."

The warm look in her eyes embarrassed Simon. "Obviously there are still flaws to be worked out. Actually…" He hesitated.

"What?"

"I was terrified it would fail and that son of a bitch was going to shoot you," he confessed.

"But it worked." She smiled at him crookedly. "My hero."

"Hardly." Now he was the one whose face was hot. "You're the one who came to my rescue."

Laura snorted. "Some rescue. I walked right into their hands."

She'd defied her boss and risked her life. For him.

"I couldn't have stopped both of them," Simon said. "You took down Vince on your own. And with your hands cuffed behind your back."

She squirmed. "That's my job."

His chest tightened with disappointment. He didn't want to be a job to her. Still…

"I'm grateful you came back to protect me," he said quietly.

Laura narrowed her eyes. "I didn't come back to protect you, you moron. I came back because I love you."

I love you.

In his whole life, no one had ever said those words to him. He would have remembered. He remembered everything now. He'd never dreamed he'd hear them for the first time from a female cop with exasperation in her voice and misery in her eyes. Or that they would fill him with such overwhelming relief. Such immeasurable joy.

He struggled for a way to tell her, but there were no words new enough or big enough, only simple words, time worn and small.

"I love you, too," he said.

Her mouth dropped open. "Oh."

His heart was beating about a million times a minute. "You said you didn't need promises. But I do. I need this one. I promise to love you for the rest of our lives if you'll let me."

She looked stunned. "Okay."

He cleared his throat, hope raking his heart. "So, it's a deal?"

"Sure."

He watched her carefully. "Want to seal it with a kiss?"

The smile he loved broke across her face and blossomed in her eyes. "Yeah."

Their lips met, touched, clung, in a kiss of breath and promise, in healing and tenderness, in communion and love.

They pulled back and smiled into one another's eyes. Kissed again, with warmth and urgency and tears and tongues.

"Ouch," Laura said.

Simon drew back instantly. "Are you all right?"

She sighed and settled her head against his shoulder. "Never better."

His good arm came around her. Carefully, because of the IV. "This isn't the most romantic setting."

"I don't need romance," Laura said. "I just need you alive and more or less in one piece."

"And in love with you," he said.

He felt her smile against his neck. "That's good, too."

And it was, he thought, tightening his arm around her. It was very good.

Chapter 17

Laura opened Simon's front door with her passcard. For the first time since her short, ill-fated marriage, she had her own key to a guy's apartment—okay, mansion—and the ordinary intimacy of it thrilled and terrified her. Even after five weeks, sharing her life and his wealth took some getting used to.

"Yo, Quinn," she called. "I'm home."

No answer.

Living with servants took some getting used to, too. Cooked meals and folded laundry were a definite plus, particularly after a day like today. But she still couldn't shake the feeling that one of these days she was going to look up from nibbling Simon's neck and lock gazes with his butler.

She shoved open the door.

No Quinn.

That was a nice surprise. Maybe Simon had given his household manager the night off. She could pay him back with a surprise of her own. Something involving bubble bath, maybe, and full frontal nudity and full penetration sex.

Smiling—she smiled a lot lately—Laura turned toward the stairs, already loosening her gun belt.

And froze with her heart in her throat.

Red. Splashes of crimson against the polished treads, going up the steps like a trail of blood.

Simon.

Not blood, she realized half a heartbeat and a hundred horrible mental scenarios later. Roses. Red rose petals, scattered on the stairs.

She took the steps two at a time, her relief morphing into confusion. What the hell was going on? Where was Simon?

She was halfway up the stairs when he appeared above her on the landing.

As always, the sight of him slapped her with a quick, visual jolt, a slow, inner melting. He was so amazingly gorgeous, the strong planes and angles of his face, his dark, thick hair, his light as rain eyes. Her wizard king. The body, in jeans and a dark T-shirt, was an added bonus.

"You're home late," he observed. "Tough day?"

"Good day." She continued toward him, shedding her tensions along with her jacket and shoes. "Chief put me on the Algonquin case. Thefts from some of the guest rooms," she explained in response to Simon's lifted eyebrows. "So I guess he's finally forgiven me for turning off my radio."

Simon frowned. "He should forgive you. He should give you a damn commendation. You broke the biggest case his department has ever seen."

"We broke the case." Reaching him, she linked her arms around his neck, loving the way his body hardened instantly against hers. "I broke protocol. But it's all right now. Kiss me."

He ran his hands possessively over her shoulders and back. But he said, "Not yet."

She scowled. She was here. She was ready. Quinn was gone. "Why not?"

Simon gave her butt a friendly squeeze and stepped back. "I have something to show you first."

"Show me later," she suggested, reaching for his buckle.

"Now," he said firmly, catching her hand and threading his fingers with hers.

"You're interfering with an officer." She pouted as he pulled her along the hall. More rose petals were strewn over the floor. It was a good thing Quinn wasn't home. He'd have a fit.

Simon slanted a look down at her. "So write me a ticket."

"I was thinking more along the lines of handcuffs. And whipped cream," she added wickedly.

"You're trying to distract me."

She grinned. "Yep. Is it working?"

"Too well." He stopped outside his bedroom door and dragged a hand through his hair. "Right. All right." He took a deep breath. "This is it."

He was nervous, she realized with tender and amused surprise. What was it? A new invention, or…?

He opened the bedroom door.

And her breath deserted her for the second time that night.

Candles gleamed from the dresser, the nightstand, the table set for two by the open French doors. Roses glowed against the silk bedspread and from heavy silver bowls and vases arranged around the room. Music played from hidden speakers.

Laura's jaw dropped. "Holy crap. What's all this?"

Simon's eyes focused on her face. "An experiment. I wanted to set the scene better this time."

She was flattered. Bewildered. Overcome. "For seduction?"

He shook his head. "For romance." He reached for a bottle chilling in the heavy silver wine cooler beside the table. "For you."

"Champagne?" Laura asked.

He smiled, lifting the bottle so she could see. Miller Genuine Draft. "I thought you might like this better."

Her hand trembled as she accepted the beer. It was too perfect. She had to take a gulp before she could speak. "I told you I don't need romance."

"Maybe you don't. Maybe I do." He opened his own bottle and raised it in a silent toast. Sipped, his eyes warm over frosted glass. "The romantically impaired and relationship challenged, isn't that how you described us?"

Her face heated. "It wasn't a criticism."

"It should have been. You deserve more. You deserve better."

She narrowed her eyes. "If you've done all this so you can tell me that one day I'll find some nice man who will love me the way I deserve to be loved, I'm going to have to hurt you."

Simon laughed. "I'm not that unselfish. No, you're stuck with me. But I can change. You taught me that."

She shook her head. "You don't need to change for me. I think you're…"

Perfect, she thought.

"Fine the way you are," she said.

"The way I am now, maybe. The way I am with you." He took her in his arms. "I want you to stay with me, Laura. I want you to marry me."

Her head was spinning. Her heart crowded her throat.

"Why me?" she asked shakily. "You're Simon Ford. You could have anyone."

He didn't argue. If he had, she could have accused him of lying.

"I don't want just anyone. I want you—your sharp mind and your fierce loyalty, your bluntness and your laughter, your grace and your strength. I need you, Laura. I love you." He took a velvet jeweler's box from its place on the table and opened it, offered it to her. "Will you marry me?"

Laura stared at the burning circlet of rubies and diamonds with the hunk of ice mounted on top. She felt as if he'd just offered her the sword in the stone, the golden apple from the tree, the happily-ever-after at the end of the fairy tale.

"Wow," she said.

Simon cleared his throat. "The rubies are the first of the Lumen Fire line."

She was still gaping at that amazing rock. It took a moment for the significance of his words to sink in. "You told Dylan yes."

Simon nodded, his eyes watchful. "He'll head the new company. Julie's already talking about jewelry design."

She beamed. "That's great."

He shrugged. "It's what he asked for."

"It's what you both need." She was no visionary genius, but she could picture how it would be, the laughter and lively arguments, the three siblings gathering around a table for business meetings or holiday dinners. "It's the family you want."

"Not quite," Simon said.

The look in his eyes made her dizzy. She forgot what they were talking about.

"You," he explained patiently. "You're the family I need. And you haven't said yes yet."

"Oh," Laura said, having a tough time forming even little words, maybe because of the beer or lack of air or just plain happiness. She took a deep breath and set down the bottle. "I... You... Yes," she said simply, and threw herself at him.

"Obviously I should have tried to romance you before," Simon murmured later. Much later. "Or was it the ring?"

"The ring is awesome. But I would have said yes without it." Laura rubbed her cheek contentedly against his chest. "I love you, Simon."

The words spilled out, she discovered, when the heart was too full to hold them.

His arms tightened around her as the candles guttered and the scent of roses filled the dark.

* * * * *

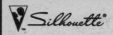
Silhouette®

INTIMATE MOMENTS™

presents a provocative new miniseries by
award-winning author

INGRID WEAVER

PAYBACK

Three rebels were brought back from the brink and
recruited into the shadowy Payback Organization.
In return for this extraordinary second chance, they
must each repay one favor in the future. But if they
renege on their promise, everything that matters
will be ripped away…including love!

Available in March 2005:

The Angel and the Outlaw
(IM #1352)

Hayley Tavistock will do anything to avenge the
murder of her brother—including forming an
uneasy alliance with gruff ex-con Cooper Webb.
With the walls closing in around them, can love
defy the odds?

Watch for Book #2 in June 2005…

Loving the Lone Wolf
(IM #1370)

Available at your favorite retail outlet.

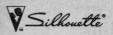

If you enjoyed what you just read,
then we've got an offer you can't resist!

Take 2 bestselling
love stories FREE!
Plus get a FREE surprise gift!

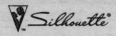

SPECIAL EDITION™

Introducing a brand-new miniseries by
Silhouette Special Edition favorite author
Marie Ferrarella

One special necklace,
three charm-filled romances!

BECAUSE A HUSBAND
IS FOREVER

by Marie Ferrarella

Available March 2005
Silhouette Special Edition #1671

Dakota Delany had always wanted a marriage like
the one her parents had, but after she found her
fiancé cheating, she gave up on love. When her
radio talk show came up with the idea of having her
spend two weeks with hunky bodyguard Ian Russell,
she protested—until she discovered she wanted Ian
to continue guarding her body forever!

Available at your favorite retail outlet.

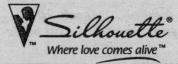

Where love comes alive™